ALSO BY MARK J. ASHER

Humphrey Was Here

A Day in Dogtown

Old Friends

Greatest Clicks

Who's That Dog?

Love For Freedom

all that ails you

The Adventures of a Canine Caregiver

A NOVEL BY MARK J. ASHER

ISBN: 978-1484834510

Printed and distributed by CreateSpace, a DBA of On-Demand Publishing, LLC

Being old isn't easy. One of the residents at SunRidge, Jane Dryden, who has since passed away, used to say the secret to having a good day was not allowing your ailments to overshadow your blessings. But there are difficult days here, when that philosophy is hard to follow or even recall. Those are the times I am needed most, when only a dog, without words, can bring love and levity to darkness and despair. You see, sometimes in life, the best thing for all that ails you has fur and four legs.

1

Moving into an assisted living home is a far cry from checking into a four-star hotel for a two-week vacation, but Walter Kepsen was in worse shape than any resident I'd ever seen arrive at SunRidge.

Some of it you could see—the way he anxiously fumbled through a stack of papers on his lap, how he quickly became exasperated when he couldn't find something in the side pocket of his scooter, and how he responded—like a threatening sky about to thunder—when Veronica broke away from their conversation to answer a phone call. But much of it, being a dog with a keen ability to detect human emotions, you could feel.

Nevertheless, always happy to see a new face, I cheerfully sauntered up to him. I sniffed around his shoe, and the tires on one side of his scooter, before I looked up, wagging, with a welcoming grin.

I might as well have been a ghost—Walter didn't acknowledge my presence with even a glance or a grunt.

I poked my nose in a few more spots, smelling nicotine on his fingers and an old blood stain on his pant leg. Once I was satisfied with my exploration, I retreated to a spot nearby, lay down, and watched as Walter and Veronica continued going over the check-in logistics.

Studying Walter from a few feet away, I realized how large a man he was. If he were standing, I imagined him to be at least six feet three inches tall. He had fingers the size of sausages, and his ears were big and doughy, like a soft pretzel. Beneath an old, worn baseball cap, he had thinning grey hair that was strewn about like a man who had spent the day sailing. His face had ruddy skin, with deep creases across his forehead, and a noticeable mole next to his nose.

I would later learn that Walter was 74, when he came to SunRidge, which made him one of the younger residents. But if you measured wear and tear versus days lived, he seemed much older.

My attention was diverted when Jane Peterson, the head Mom, and owner of SunRidge, came up to greet Walter. Her sunny disposition did nothing to ease the scowl on Walter's face. The two of them made forced conversation for a minute, before Jane led Walter to his new room. I followed alongside.

There's always an adjustment period with each new resident, in which I learn about their personalities, temperament, mental capacity, and physical limitations. Walter wasted no time in defining his preference as it related to me.

"What's with the dog?" he barked, glaring down at me, as we approached his room.

"That's Wrigley, our house dog," Jane answered, looking over at me with a smile.

"Get him away, will you. No one told me there was a dog here."

"Wrigley, go on, scoot!" Jane commanded me, with unusual emphasis.

From trailing Father McMahon during his visits to SunRidge, in hopes of getting one of the liver treats he often kept in his front right pocket, I know the bible says: *Forgive them, for they know not what they do.* But after being around seniors for a while, I picked my spots to adopt the philosophy of: *Ignore them, for they know not what they need.* So in that spirit, I gave Walter a quick lick on his hand before heading to see Marjorie Thompson, across the hall.

The door was slightly ajar, which was Marjorie's signal to me that it was okay to enter. I nudged it open with my snout, walked inside, and found Marjorie fast asleep on her recliner. I made my usual rounds, sniffing for anything new, and glancing out the window before settling on the floor nearby. As I was dozing off, I heard Jane saying goodbye to Walter.

"Can I get you anything else, Walter?" she asked him.

"Yeah, get me out of here. I can't believe my son took me out of a perfectly fine apartment, and left me to die in a dump like this."

"It might take a while, Walter, but we'll do our best to make this feel like home," Jane assured him.

"You can start by moving that chair," Walter instantly replied. "I don't like where it is, I can't see outside."

"No problem," Jane responded, now standing in the doorway. "I'll have it taken care of by the end of today."

Carla Swenson, a caregiver, who worked the 6:00am to 2:30pm shift, was the next SunRidge employee I saw encounter Walter. She had the personality of a Lab—happy-go-lucky, jovial and accommodating. There wasn't a resident that didn't adore her.

I was lying in my familiar spot—just inside of Marjorie's doorway—when Carla walked into Walter's room.

"Whatever you're selling, I don't want any," I heard Walter say, before Carla could say hello.

"I'm not here to sell you anything," Carla replied.

"Then get the hell out of here."

"It'll just take a minute," Carla told Walter. "I need to draw some blood."

"Can't you see I'm watching a game right now?" he responded.

"You can watch your game, while I do my job."

"What exactly is your job?"

"Didn't anybody tell you?" Carla asked playfully, trying to draw Walter in.

"No," Walter grunted.

"I'm the local vampire who comes to suck your blood."

There was silence for a second, and then I heard Walter reply, "Well, it's been long time since I've had a woman suck anything of mine, so go ahead. Just don't block the TV."

Carla had a bemused expression on her face, when she left Walter's room, and came over to rub my head.

As you might have figured, Walter didn't last very long as the new resident who nobody knew. That night in the dining room, while everyone was eating, the rumble of human chatter and the sound of metal utensils against plates came to a sudden halt.

"This meat loaf is terrible!" Walter blurted out, before throwing his utensils and napkin down on his plate, and pushing himself away from the table.

You could have heard a pin drop. As he grabbed his cane and left the dining room, every head in the place, including the kitchen staff, looked over at Walter.

Thankfully, Sandi Schifman broke the silence.

"Well, I think everything tastes just delicious . . . and I intend to enjoy every bite of it," she said, allowing conversation in the dining room to slowly resume.

5

I watched Walter as he made his way past me. I waited for a few moments at the periphery of the dining room, and then followed him at a distance. When he arrived at his room, out of view from everyone but me, I discovered that he hadn't entirely disliked his meal. As he reached into his pant pocket for his room key, three wheat rolls fell from beneath his sweater. He picked up two, but missed one, which bounced behind him. When he closed the door, I confiscated the remaining wheat roll faster than you could say *hypocrite*.

A few days later, I was walking by Walter's room when I heard a loud grunting noise. I poked my head inside the partially opened door, and didn't see him in the entryway or in the living room. My nose lured me to his couch where I found a nice-sized piece of turkey in between the cracks of the cushions. Feeling lucky, I doubled back to the kitchen to search for scraps. There were a lot of smells, but nothing noteworthy in the corners or crevices. When I went to sniff under the refrigerator, I heard the loud noise again.

I followed it into the adjoining room, made a quick right turn, and found Walter sitting on the toilet with his eyes closed. I leaned my head down and sniffed between his legs.

"Jesus Christ!" he yelled. "Get the hell out of here!"

I must not have found the exit fast enough, because Walter swatted me with his cane, catching me on my butt.

6

In my time as the house dog at SunRidge, I'd been squeezed tightly, cried on, prayed to, slept on, but never hit. It caused me to do something I hadn't done since I was a puppy.

I quickly darted back toward Walter, grabbed the top sheet of toilet paper from the dispenser with my mouth, and ran with it a few feet. As I left the room, I heard him mumbling something to himself. There would be no parting lick this time.

Over the next year and a half there were a lot of twists and turns before Walter passed away. If you would have told me half of what happened, I would have thought that you had snuck into the medication room and misread the dosing instructions on a bottle of Demerol.

2

I didn't start my life out at an assisted living home. I came to SunRidge shortly after Jane Peterson adopted me, when I was six years old.

Initially, I lived at the Peterson house with Jane, her husband, Ron, and their daughters, Theresa and Tamara. But running SunRidge is a family business, so they brought me to work with them often. Before long, the residents began to grow attached to me.

The seniors liked the idea of having something soft, cheerful, and comforting around. I quickly realized that old people had two things that every dog craves: time and love. It wasn't long before I became the official, full-time house dog.

I know what you might be thinking—wouldn't a dog rather be living with a young family with two energetic kids and a large backyard?

One of the attributes of being a dog is not living in the past. I'm grateful for that because mine is a painful one.

For the first six years of my life, I went from home to home, with depressing stays in-between at the shelter. I've been everything from Bart to Bartholomew. I figure by now I've had as many names as a call girl with a long career.

The unfortunate part is that I'm a good dog—smart, cute, and mostly well-behaved. Sadly, sometimes a good dog can have bad luck, and that's my story. On the positive side, like many dogs who've had a hard go, I'm as sweet as sugar with none of the side effects.

Breed wise, I'm a mix of many things, my best guess is German shepherd, Husky, and maybe some Lab. My coat is brown and black, and I weigh 45 pounds. People always comment on my widow's peak, which makes me look sweet and gives me character. My most unusual feature has to be my tail because it's disproportionately large in relation to the rest of my body.

My first home was on an old cherry farm in Emmett, Idaho. It was a wonderful place to be a puppy—lots of open space with room to roam and fresh scents to smell.

But while the nature was plentiful, the owners were pitiful. The family didn't give me any love or training, and the youngest son liked to do cruel experiments on me when he got bored.

I don't know if the parents found out or they just got tired of me, but six months later, I was given to another family down the road. I lasted there for a little less than a year before I was put in a crate, loaded in the back of a truck, and taken on a long ride. It turned out to be a one way trip to an animal shelter just outside of Boise.

It was hard and strange to go from spending my days in the country, where there weren't any restrictions, to a small, confined concrete box.

Shelter life doesn't take long to figure out. You quickly realize there are only two ways out: the front gate, which leads to a new life or the back door, which leads to death. You spend your days hoping that someone looking for a new dog will take notice of you. If they do, they'll ask to take you out to one of the outdoor runs for a meet and greet. If you're lucky, they'll take you home and give you a new life. If you get adopted by a good owner or family, you're golden and set for life. But, if you get a bad one, most likely you'll end up back on death row.

Unfortunately, I know the latter scenario all too well. The first time I got adopted was by the Phelps Family, who had two young kids: Jake and Jesse. I was overjoyed to be free again and belong to a new pack.

It was my first experience being around kids, and I happily discovered they're just like dogs—the first thing on their minds is fun, and the last thing they want to do is follow the rules. We had a great time together, hanging out, playing games, and visiting the neighbors across the street, who had a super-friendly St. Bernard named Conroy. During the summertime, the parents took the kids and me camping on the weekends to great spots with mountains, meadows, and streams, where we could run free and play.

Heartbreakingly, over time, the family began to fall into financial trouble. Eventually, they were forced to move out of their home into an apartment, which didn't allow dogs. It was a bad break and a real crusher, because I felt I had finally found my place in the world.

If by chance I come back in my next life as a human, I'm definitely going to build a huge apartment complex that only allows people *with* dogs.

Whether I liked it or not, I was back in solitary confinement at the same crappy shelter. Luckily, it only took a few months for another couple—this one without kids—to adopt me.

Tracie and Norm fought like cats and dogs, day and night. For the life of me, I couldn't understand why two people would stay in the same place when they couldn't stand one another. But I'm a dog—when we don't like one of our own kind, we might tussle a bit, but eventually we go off and find a different dog to play with.

Tracie loved me; Norm hated me. When he wasn't around, she would love me like her first born, pampering me with toys and treats, and anything else my nose gravitated to along the pet store aisle. When she wasn't around, he would drink like a dog with a chunk of peanut butter stuck to the roof of its mouth. Afterward, he would get agitated and angry. I didn't have to do much to earn a swat from a rolled up magazine, or on a bad day, the TV remote.

I never snapped at him, but I wasn't above subtle revenge. At night when Norm used to take his socks off, and leave them on the floor beside the bed, I would move them into the exercise room or the living room. It drove him crazy. I can still hear him yelling to Tracie in the morning, when he woke up, "Where the hell are my socks?"

I was living with this dysfunctional duo for seven months before a neighbor spotted Norm spraying me with the garden hose, and reported the incident to animal services.

To be honest, the reason Norm was spraying me was I had become interested in a strange scent in the backyard. At first taking a few sniffs sufficed, but I quickly realized this was a scent that had to be savored. So, I rolled onto my back and squirmed all over it, wildly flailing my legs in the air. I couldn't get enough—the second I got back on my feet, I had the irresistible urge to rub on the scent again. When Norm got a whiff of me, he became enraged, ranting about what a horrible dog I was, before spraying me like a civil rights demonstrator in Selma, Alabama.

When I arrived at the shelter again, I was relieved to be out of a bad situation, but depressed to be put in cage 39, all the way at the end of the row. Being toward the back of the building means you get far less visitors, which increases your chances of getting put down. Instead of lying on your bed and waiting for people to walk by—like you can do in the better spots—you spend most of the day standing, and hoping that someone glances down the walkway and takes an interest in you.

Being an older dog now, I began to worry about my chances of getting adopted. In a world with more dogs than there are owners to love them, age is a liability.

I had this one couple who was super interested in me. After our initial visit, they even returned the next day with their chocolate Lab, Jeremy, so I could meet him. We got along great, but eventually the woman turned to her husband and said, "Let's go see some of the other ones, I don't know if I want an older dog." I never saw them again.

This is one of the toughest parts about being a shelter dog—meeting people that seem promising, but for what-ever reason, don't pan out. In most cases, you get five minutes, sometimes more, sometimes less, in a small out-door pen to sell yourself. On some visits, you're so happy just to be free from confinement that you spend the entire time running around like a wild man or jumping all over your potential savior, desperate for attention.

Thankfully, in a few more months, after two short stints as a foster, Jane Peterson showed up at my cage to say hello. She spoke to me in a comforting, soft voice, while poking her fingers through the cage to scratch behind my ears. Sensing she was a good candidate, I did my best to charm her by cocking my head to her questions, and rubbing myself back and forth against the metal door.

With Jane, I instantly knew I had her, and she had me. A few minutes into our visit, she turned to one of the volunteers and said, "This is the one."

Rachel, my favorite shelter employee, took me back to my cement block to grab a squeaky toy I had become attached to, and then we quickly walked past the boisterous serenade of barking dogs, toward the administration building. Jane was waiting for us inside, where she was finishing up the paperwork.

Hopping into the front seat of her minivan, I had no idea where the next stop in my journey would take me. I only hoped it would be my last one.

3

I still remember the first time the Petersons brought me to SunRidge. My senses were on overload with so much to smell—medicine, medical equipment, wheelchairs, walkers, canes, and so many people to see—caregivers, kitchen staff, cleaning crew, and delivery people.

Then, of course, there were the residents. Forty-five of them to be exact. Each of their rooms was a treasure trove of time-worn odors, knickknacks, keepsakes, and other oddities collected over a lifetime. Like people themselves, no two rooms were alike. Each had its own personal style and feel.

I was amazed by how many seniors had stuffed animals. Who knew that old people had enough plush teddy bears, pigs, and monkeys to open a large toy store? Being a dog who loves them, I assumed they were mine for the taking. But after I ate Lola Gladlock's elephant, Foster, and got a serious reprimand, I learned they weren't.

Many of the seniors had a family member buy a dog bed to put in their room, so I would be comfortable and stay longer. It became a competition of sorts to see which spot I liked the most. They were all fine by me, but my favorite resident, Marjorie Thompson, had the best one. It was a large mound of mushiness, and every time I collapsed on it, I felt like I was lying on a cloud.

Treats, of course, were another incentive to keep me around. Some of the residents kept them in their memento boxes, beside their doors, or in jars on their kitchen counters. Peanut butter biscuits are my absolute favorite, but I'll happily crunch on anything edible.

I spent a lot of my time visiting with residents in their rooms, but the center of activity at SunRidge was in the large living room, and in an adjoining restaurant-style dining room.

Unfortunately, the better smelling of the two was off limits to me. I faithfully stayed behind an imaginary line, bordering the dining room, which Jane had trained me not to cross. Sometimes, I would sit and wait for the residents to finish their meals. But having a sense of smell a thousand times greater than humans do, and watching a room full of seniors eating can be pure torture. Imagine being a dog and seeing an 86 year old woman enjoying a piece of chicken in a slow motion, and having to contain yourself from running over, jumping up, and ripping the chicken right from her fork.

That's why most times, after a short while, I would retreat to my bed beside Theresa Peterson's desk, in one of the front offices, next to the reception area. She and Jane were the ones who fed me, gave me my daily walks, and took care of most of the obligatory dog owner respon-sibilities. Ron and Tamara, who shared the office next-door, also pitched in to love and care for me.

The living room was a social gathering spot where the residents schmoozed with friends and family, attended events, or just relaxed. Open and inviting, the space was filled with couches, cushy chairs, a TV, and a great fire-place. The centerpiece of the room was a beautiful grand piano. Ron Peterson, who liked to play, often joined a group of visiting musicians to entertain the seniors.

The most unique part of the living room was a large fish tank, which was filled with an assortment of colorful characters. There was a particularly plump one with buggy eyes, who always stared at me like he wanted to play chase, if he could only break out of the glass tank.

SunRidge had other spots as well, where the residents spent their time, and where I wandered in and out on a daily basis. There was an entertainment room with a large-screen TV for movies; an activity room for Bingo, scrapbooking, arts and crafts, and various classes and clubs; a library, and even a beauty salon.

My favorite place was the courtyard. It was my piece of paradise, where I could sit in the grass and take in the fresh air, mill about, and chase balls. During the wintertime, I had the whole area to myself. When the weather was warm, the residents joined me, and sat in rocking chairs, which were shaded from the sun by the building's overhang, or beneath the large gazebo in the center of the courtyard.

Unfortunately, one of my favorite outdoor activities— chasing squirrels—was a limited occurrence. There were spurts when I would see a couple of them, and then long spells with no sightings. Something about the way the courtyard was enclosed, or perhaps how the landscaping was maintained, must have kept them away.

It's a shame, because as a dog, there's nothing like the thrill of trying to catch a squirrel. It starts the second you hear one chirping, or you get a glimpse of those beady, black eyes. Then the stalking phase begins, as you watch them with baited breath, while they lilt and scurry about. When you can't stand their arrogant, carefree demeanor a second longer, you explode in a full blown sprint for prey. If you're really lucky, you'll nab the bushy-tailed buggard, and not get stuck looking up a tree, barking in vain, while your menace dances from limb to limb in taunting glee. But I suppose you'd need to have an undomesticated past to truly appreciate any of this.

For the majority of my time at SunRidge, I've been the only dog. But there have been a few of them that have come and gone. My favorite of all was a small black Lab mix named Satchmo. He was a clown of a dog, always doing something to make the humans laugh.

When Satchmo's owner, Bob Sanderson, passed, there was some talk about keeping him as a second house dog. Jane was open to the idea, wanting to keep Satchmo in a familiar environment, and not wanting to abandon an eight year old dog. But Ron felt that the dog was not well enough trained in that capacity to be around seniors. He told Jane that Satchmo only responded to reverse-action training— when you say *leave it*, he eats it. As it turned out, a friend of Tamara Peterson gave Satch a great home.

Several of the residents had cats, but they steered clear of me. I'd see them peek out of their owner's rooms, only to quickly scurry back inside whenever I got close. I remember hearing the Phelps' kids using the term *scaredy cat*—now I know where it comes from.

I felt sorry for the residents with cats. A cat's company, compared to that of a dog, is not much more comforting than having a pet rock, and in choosing to have a cat they missed out on visits from the house dog.

I can't say much about the décor at SunRidge, because dogs have no expertise in interior design, except for spotting cozy couches. Not to mention, our perception of colors is limited. But I will say the Peterson family worked hard to make it a friendly, homey place that felt like a big country house. It didn't change some of the hard realities the residents faced in the final stage of their lives, but it made for a loving, positive environment.

4

I was completely content one summer afternoon, lying in a patch of sunlight that was streaming through the window, when I heard Marjorie say, "Look, Wrigley."

I sprang up and looked outside, spotting a young girl playing with her yellow Lab puppy, in the backyard across the way. The house had been up for sale and empty for a long time, but over the last week a new family had begun to move in.

I watched with jealousy and intrigue, as the dog chased the girl back and forth alongside a Slip 'n Slide. His tongue was dangling, and his body was soaking wet.

"That sure looks like fun, doesn't it, Wrigley?" Marjorie said, turning to me. "I bet you'd like to be out there."

When the two finally got tuckered out, they lay together on the grass; the dog on its side, panting rapidly in the heat, and the girl on her back, with the sun glistening off her wet skin.

Marjorie swallowed a couple of pills with a sip of water, and then stared out the window for a long while.

"I can still remember being that age," she said, finally breaking her silence. "It feels like it'll last forever. But before you know it, the pages of your life start to fly by. You wake up one day and you're a grown woman, then a wife and a mother, then a grandmother, and gradually, then suddenly, an old lady like me. It all happens so fast."

The young girl and the dog got up from their short rest and were back at it again, slipping and sliding, with water flying all over both of them.

"It's a funny thing about life," Marjorie continued, as I situated myself beside her chair to solicit affection, "the good old days never seem as good until they get old. The struggles of life fade and leave sweet memories. If only we could appreciate the time we have, while we're living it."

As the house dog, I didn't have a set schedule—I went where I sensed I was needed. But every dog has their favorites, and Marjorie Johnson was mine.

It's been that way since the first time we met, not long after I began making visits here. She was playing Bingo with a group of ladies, and I went straight to her side. When the game was over, I followed Marjorie back to her room. We sat together for hours, strangers to one another, but connected in the magical way a dog bonds with a human, when it finds a kindred spirit.

Even though she was 87 years old and struggling with a series of medical issues, beneath her fragile frame, trembling hands, and weathered skin, Marjorie was still an excitable little girl. I couldn't understand all of her life experiences, but I enjoyed listening to her talk, and always loved her company.

She came to SunRidge after her husband, Frank, passed away. She picked up a photograph of him, either in the living room or from her nightstand, at least once a day, and spoke to him. I feel that I know Frank through all the stories I've heard about their lives together.

When the girl and her dog went inside the house, Marjorie picked up the sweater she had been working on for her great-granddaughter and began to knit. Before she could finish a stitch, there was a knock on the door, and Carla, the caregiver, came into the room.

She walked over and put her arm around Marjorie's shoulder, and then leaned over and patted my head.

"Miss Marjorie, it looks like you're in good company," she said, while putting a few things down on the end table beside the couch.

"We're just talking about life. Right, Wrigley?" Marjorie replied, smiling at me.

"With a dog, huh?" Carla said with a laugh.

"Well, I know they can't offer any words of wisdom, but they sure are comforting to be around."

"I'm with you. Sometimes late at night, after my son's gone to bed, I sit and have the best conversations of my day with our Golden, Smitty."

I looked up at both of them, my tail wagging back and forth like a metronome.

"He must know we're talking about his kind," Carla said to Marjorie, looking down at me. She then walked over to the jar on the kitchen counter, and grabbed a peanut butter biscuit. I wasn't far behind.

"Does this sweet boy want a treat?" she asked, turning to face me. I gave her my paw, and she reciprocated by handing me the biscuit.

I happily brought it back over to where Marjorie was sitting, and broke it into two pieces, before finishing it off.

While the ladies continued to chat, Marjorie turned on *Animal Planet*. Unless there was something earth-shattering going on in the world, we always watched it whenever I was in her room.

Not surprisingly, it's my favorite channel on TV. However, if anyone associated with the show is reading this, I do have two suggestions. First, replace all of the cat programs with dog programs. There simply isn't that much to say about cats, other than they are aloof and mostly selfish creatures. Secondly, cut down on the number of dog food commercials. Until someone invents a television, where you can smell and taste what you see, it's simply one tease after another, without any reward.

Other than that, though, the shows are fantastic.

This one was on the science of dogs. The narrator was talking about a powerful hormone called Oxytocin, which human mothers release when they breastfeed their babies. It creates a bond between the mother and her child. For an experiment, the researchers tested dogs and their human companions, after they spent time together, to see how their levels of Oxytocin were affected. Incredibly, Oxytocin rose in both the dogs and their owners, the same way it does with human mothers and their newborns. Powerful stuff, don't you think?

During a car commercial, I looked over at Marjorie and Carla, and they were still talking.

"I heard that crotchety old man across the way gave you a hard time the other day," Marjorie said.

"He can be a cranky one, that's for sure," Carla responded.

"Did I tell you about our exchange the other day?"

"No."

"Well, I was coming out of my room and he was coming out of his. I said 'Good morning' and he grunted 'It's morning all right, but I don't know if it's good. What's so good about waking up old, achy, and irritable in a place like this?' And then he mumbled off."

"I wonder if he's ever been married," Carla asked.

"Misery loves company, but I just can't imagine who would want to be with that man," Marjorie answered, before pausing. "Oh, I know that's a terrible thing to say, but he just strikes me as the type of person who likes to create clouds in their life, and then gets angry when it rains."

"Jane keeps telling me to give him a chance—that he'll adjust. She said a relative of Walter's called to check on him, and told her he's got a heart of gold."

"If he's got a heart of gold, Carla, I'm afraid you're going to have to get past the angry man who's guarding it first."

Before I turned back to the TV, Marjorie got up, walked over to the kitchen counter, and picked up a small vase filled with cut flowers. "I know you hate birthdays," she told Carla, while handing her the fragrant bouquet, "but I thought you might like these."

"Thank you, but you really shouldn't have."

"I know you told me, but I forget . . . why don't you like birthdays?" Marjorie asked.

"They remind me of where I'm at in my life."

"Young, smart, and beautiful," Marjorie said, smiling.

"Hardly... No, I really want my son to have a father figure in his life, and at the rate I'm going, it doesn't seem likely."

"You'll find someone again, and this time it won't be a creep."

"I feel bad that he doesn't have what other kids have."

"You mean a Dad?"

"That and the financial means to do some of the things the other kids can do. I work hard to keep him in a good school, but we're one of the only families who don't have money."

"Is Dylan happy?" Marjorie asked.

"I think so. I just wish I could give him more."

"As parents, we always do," Marjorie replied. "Listen, Carla, he may not have everything you want him to have, but the most important thing is that he knows he's rich with love. You're a great mother. Don't discount that."

"I knew there was a good reason I always look forward to seeing you," Carla replied. "I've got to get going, but thank you again for the flowers. I have the perfect place for them."

When Carla turned to leave, I followed her, hoping she'd decide to give me a parting treat. Instead, I settled for a sympathetic smile and a quick head rub.

When she opened the door, Walter was sitting in his red scooter, in the middle of the hallway, with a scowl on his face. It turned out he was waiting for his son, Mark, who was coming down the corridor.

After Carla waved goodbye to Marjorie, and excused herself, I took to my perch inside the doorway.

"I was wondering when you'd get here," Walter scoffed when Mark reached him.

"Sorry, you're not the only obligation in my life," Mark responded, annoyed by his father's welcome.

"Listen, get me out of this place, I can't stand it," Walter told his son. "The food, the people, the room…everything."

"Dad, you can't fend for yourself any longer, and you don't have the money to hire people to take care of you."

"My luck, I come down to the end of my life, and lose almost everything I have in a God-damn Ponzi scheme."

"You're not the only one who lost money; we all did," Mark replied. "I realize it's not a good situation, but life goes on."

"For you maybe," Walter snapped.

"Some life… I either feel guilty that I'm not doing enough for you or resentful that I spend as much time helping you as I do."

Mark looked at Walter for a moment without saying anything. You could see he felt bad about his harsh tone.

"Dad, it's not that bad of a place," he reasoned. "I have a friend who told me her mother got great care here. She also said there's three times as many women as men. Who knows, maybe you'll find someone nice."

"Just what I need after 25 years of marriage to your mother, and then this last nightmare—another broad."

"I don't know what else you want me to say," Mark replied, exasperated. "You'll adjust."

"All right, let's not talk about it anymore."

"You never want to talk about anything, you just like to

complain. And I don't have the time or the energy to listen to it."

"Then get the hell out of here, and leave me alone."

With that, Mark turned and left SunRidge.

5

After Mark left, and Walter returned to his room, Marjorie gathered a few things and made her way to the activity room to play Bingo. She went whenever she felt up to it, and always looked forward to spending time with her close group of lady friends. Whenever we were together, I would tag along.

From a dog's perspective, Bingo rates up there as one of the most tedious ways humans choose to pass their time. But, if SunRidge dared to skip one of the three scheduled weekly games, they would get a great deal of grief from several of the residents.

Despite my feelings about the game, Marjorie always added a twist that made it fun for me. Alongside her card, she played a special card for me that had the word "TREAT" in large letters beneath the "BINGO" heading. If I won, she'd call TREAT, and I'd race to Tamara, the social coordinator, who called the numbers, to collect my prize. Usually it was a small rawhide twist or a heart-shaped treat.

Like everyone who plays Bingo, you need luck to win. So on this afternoon, I lay at Marjorie's feet, falling in and out of sleep, listening to the ladies talk about their lives and the latest gossip, while I waited for my good fortune to strike.

At one point, I heard Marjorie telling her friends about the argument Walter had with his son in the hallway. The consensus of the group was that Walter wouldn't last much longer at SunRidge. However, one lady, Louise Brooks, shocked everyone when she confessed that although Walter acted like a brute, she found him to be attractive in a way she couldn't describe.

"Call me crazy," she said, "but I think there's a soft side to him."

To which Mary Jo Pickerton quickly responded, "Didn't Hitler have one as well?"

The ladies all laughed.

"I was excited when I saw that another male was moving in," Evelyn Michaels chimed in from the next table over. "So much for that."

"What's the difference?" Estelle Hadley asked. "Most of them just want to be taken care of, and I'm done with that."

I waited and waited, but it wasn't my lucky day for Bingo. Joan Mangini looked over at me, sensing my boredom, and said, "Poor sweetheart hasn't won anything yet today."

"Maybe he just needs to cross his paws," Mary Jo said with a laugh. "That's what my sweet old dog, Rusty used to like to do. Cutest thing in the world."

I decided to get up and head back to the front office. I was halfway there, when I smelled ginger cookies in the air! Jamie, the kitchen manager, baked them every so often in the afternoons for the residents. The occasion was the one exception to the dining room boundary line, and it always got me super-excited.

"How's my good buddy doing today?" Jamie asked, noticing me standing near the doorway leading to the kitchen.

Dogs respond to enthusiasm, and Jamie never had a shortage of it.

"You smelled something good, didn't you boy?" he said, patting my mid-section like we were football teammates.

I sat down and made my body rigid as a soldier about to say, *Yes sir!*

"I know these are your favorites," he said, while walking back over to the cookie tray on the counter.

One thing about Jamie—he could be a bit long-winded before delivering the goods.

"Well, let's just see what we've got here."

I inched a few feet closer, licking my chops.

"They sure smell good."

Jamie touched one of the cookies to see if they were ready.

"Just a little bit longer, Wrigley . . . I don't want you to burn your tongue."

Don't worry about my tongue, Jamie—that cookie is going straight to my stomach.

Finally, a minute later, Jamie walked over with a cookie in his hand. He broke it in half, and gave me the larger piece. I half-chewed it before quickly swallowing, so I could get the rest of the cookie. Jamie knew me well.

"Okay, Wrigley, but just one more piece and that's it."

He handed me the other half without delay.

Even though Jamie never gave me more than one cookie, I always sat and stared at him, hoping to guilt him into changing his mind. When it proved futile, I would intently watch him scrape the cookies from the tray onto a plate, and then follow him, sniffing all the way, as he set them out for the residents and staff to enjoy.

After my dinner that evening, I followed Tamara around, as she made preparations for one of the more popular events on the SunRidge social calendar—movie night. It took place every Saturday night at 6:30pm in the entertainment room. My unofficial, self-assigned role on these occasions was as greeter and popcorn eater.

When the time came, I stood at the door of the

33

entertainment room, as the residents filed in, welcoming them with sniffs and kisses, and getting rubs and scratches in return. After everyone was seated, I milled about, visiting with a few of the residents who wanted more of my company.

While Ann Hanrady was telling me about her last dog—a bulldog named Seymour—I looked up and was surprised to see Walter slowly make his way into the room. He took a seat in the back row, and sat stoically, waiting for the movie to begin. I didn't think of approaching him, and from what I saw, nobody else did either.

My socializing phase abruptly came to an end, as it always did on movie nights, when I heard the first pop coming from the microwave in the back of the room. I rushed over and began dancing on my hind legs, next to Tamara, while she stood waiting for the popcorn to be ready.

"Ladies and gentlemen…" she announced, looking at me, and then back at the residents, "For your pre-movie entertainment, I present to you, Wrigley, the dancing dog."

The residents clapped and laughed.

"Go, Wrigley, go," I heard one of them yell out.

"He's a regular Fred Astaire," another one said.

"He beats watching previews any day," Marjorie added.

When the microwave stopped, Tamara divvied up the popcorn into small bowls to those who wanted some. She never gave me any, because she knew I would make the rounds and sit beside the most generous seniors, who were willing to share a few kernels of joy, and that I would happily help myself to any popcorn that accidently ended up on the floor.

Marjorie was always my first stop, and she didn't disappoint. After I tried my luck with a few others, I looked up and met eyes with Walter, who was consuming a rather large portion of popcorn. His menacing glare was unambiguous. It clearly said: *Don't even think about it, dog.*

Realizing there was no more good stuff to get, I found a comfortable spot on the ground next to Marjorie, and drifted off to sleep. Once in a while, if the movie had an animal prominently featured in it, I'd watch, but most times I'd close my eyes and hope to dream of chasing a squirrel through a forest with no trees.

After the film ended—this one was *As Good As It Gets*—there was a short discussion amongst Tamara and the residents.

Although Walter never said much to the other residents at SunRidge, he wasn't shy about giving his opinion on whatever came to his mind.

"Now, there's a realistic premise," he said sarcastically, soon after the conversation began. "A pretty, young blonde falls for an old curmudgeon."

"I really enjoyed it," Dolores Johnson said.

"Leave it to a woman to believe sap like that," Walter

responded.

"Helen Hunt and Jack Nicholson did win Academy awards for Best Actress and Best Actor for their performances," Tamara, the film buff of the bunch, added.

"Who cares, it's completely unrealistic," Walter rebutted.

"For goodness sake, Walter, it's a movie," Marjorie chimed in. "What's life without fantasies and dreams?"

"It's called reality," Walter cracked. "You might try it sometime."

A dog can do many things, and mediating is one of them. I waited for a couple more verbal volleys to go back and forth between Walter and the others in the group, before I began to whimper.

"Sounds like Wrigley wants to add something to the discussion," Dolores said, smiling.

I whimpered again, this time paddling my front paws in the air and landing on the side of Marjorie's chair.

"What is it, sweet boy?" she asked me.

"I think he's asking, 'Are you positive there's no more popcorn?'" Tamara said with laugh.

"Dumb dog probably just needs to take a piss," Walter blurted out.

Wouldn't it be funny, I thought, if I sheepishly walked over, lifted my leg, and spritzed on Walter's scooter by the door. That would give him the satisfaction of being right.

As it was, my whimpering did the trick. The bickering

36

ended, and Walter left the room, while a group of ladies went on talking about their favorite male actors.

6

It didn't take long for Walter to wear out his welcome with Carla, or any of her fellow caregivers for that matter. She requested—insisted might be a more accurate way of putting it—to have someone else care for him. Everyone has a breaking point, no matter how tolerant or kind, and Carla had reached hers.

Theresa was cutting my nails, when Carla came into the front office one afternoon visibly upset.

"I can't take that man for a minute more!" she cried. "He's intolerable, he's rude, and he's impossible to please."

"Carla, try to calm down and tell me what happened," Jane said from her desk.

"Walter called me a worthless piece of shit, because I

put his water down where he didn't want it."

As the conversation continued, I could sense Jane and Theresa were finding it difficult to respond. They were caught between caring for a resident—no matter how ornery—and keeping the sanity of one of their favorite caregivers.

"He needs a robot, not a caregiver. Find someone else," Carla said, adamantly, having no such dilemma.

With that, Carla turned and stormed out of the office. Theresa started to get up to go after her, but Jane motioned to leave her be.

I felt bad for Carla. I observed her and the rest of the caregivers on a daily basis, and it was impossible not to admire them. The residents depended on them to do the simple things they could no longer do for themselves, and they did it with smiles on their faces, and love in their hearts. These were angels who deserved to be appreciated, not belittled.

I waited for Theresa to finish fiddling with my nails, and then left the room to follow Carla's scent. It led me to—of all places—one of the storage rooms. The door was open wide enough for me to slip through, and I found her sitting on a stack of boxes. Her head was buried in her hands. She didn't feel my presence, until I licked her elbow.

Without saying anything, she lifted her hands away from her eyes. Then, she began slowly stroking my ears back, over and over again. After several minutes, her tears stopped and she gave me a faint smile.

"I got into this profession to help people," she told me, looking exhausted, "but I'm learning that some people don't want your help. They just want you to be a punching bag for all of their frustrations."

I lay down beside her, and listened as she continued to vent. When she got everything out of her system, she looked down at me and said, "I wish I were a dog today, Wrigley. I just feel like falling asleep in the sun and forgetting about life for a while. But I guess it's time to go out and face the world again."

I don't know if Jane forced it upon Walter or he took it upon himself, but a few days later there were a pair of private caregivers taking care of him. A stocky man named Rudy Hemen helped a few hours during the day, and a young Filipina woman named Corina Navarro assisted Walter in the evening. They seemed pleasant enough, but both were cool when it came to their enthusiasm for the house dog.

Unfortunately, neither one of them was able to perform any magic on Walter's disposition. He was still the same cantankerous and contentious person he had been since arriving at SunRidge.

It didn't take long for Corina to realize what she was in for.

One evening, shortly after she began working for Walter, a new resident named Ruth Redderson tripped and fell in the hallway. I was resting inside of Marjorie's doorway when it happened, and went over to lick up some of the milk, which Ruth had spilled on her sweater and pants.

Walter's door was open at the time, and Corina—having heard the fall—walked out to assist the resident. She helped Ruth to her feet, and then retrieved a towel from Walter's room to clean up the mess.

When Corina returned to Walter's room, she got her first taste of his prickly nature.

"What were you doing out there?" I heard him ask, insistently.

"A woman fell, I was helping her up," Corina replied.

"Listen, when you're here, you work for me," he said sternly. "Do you understand?"

"But, I was just helping…"

"I don't care what you were doing," Walter responded sharply, cutting Corina off. "When you're here, you work for me."

When I went back to Marjorie's room, she was standing in her doorway, having listened to the altercation.

"What a selfish, old fool," she said, disgusted. "He had better get used to this place, because God keeps people like him around until they learn the lesson of kindness."

7

Over the next couple of weeks Walter kept a low profile, and although I saw him once in a while, he spent most of his time in his room with the door closed. He didn't partake in one of the most out of the ordinary events I can remember at SunRidge.

I was fast asleep in front of the fireplace in the living room, when I heard the sound of chairs moving. As I opened my eyes, I saw a few of the staff members preparing the space for guests. Standing off to the side, waiting for things to be set up, were two local newspaper reporters, who had come to interview the seniors for a story on how they felt about today's culture.

I got up and greeted the young woman and man with

excitement and curiosity, poking my wet nose around their briefcases, notebooks, and recording equipment. They tolerated my invasion with smiles and pats on my head.

As I began shifting my attention from the reporters to the arriving seniors, I picked up Marjorie's scent, and looked around until I spotted her coming into the room to join the group.

"How's my sweet boy doing?" she asked, when I went over to her.

I wagged and wiggled and panted, seeing her for the first time all day.

She reached her hand into a large bag at her side, and I sensed a surprise.

"Look what one of my grandchildren got for you," she said, holding up a monkey for me to see.

I took the monkey by the tail with my mouth, and tossed him in the air to myself a few times, before following Marjorie to find a place to sit in the front row.

While I became acquainted with my new friend, which it turned out, had no stuffing, but instead, a plastic bottle for a body, Marjorie made small talk with a few of the residents. After all of the seniors had filed into the room and were seated, the reporters got everyone's attention, and introduced themselves as Randi Reese and Tim Kellerman. As they began to explain the impetus for their story, and the objective for the discussion, Sandi Schifman interrupted and joked, "So, you want to hear how we all

43

walked to school in the snow, right?" The reporters chuckled and smiled, and then began to ask the residents a series
of questions.

The seniors, some of whom were born before
electricity, and all who had experienced life-altering
inventions like the television and the automobile, gave the
reporters an earful on how they viewed the fast-changing
world.

I drifted in and out of sleep, repositioned myself often,
stretched, yawned, and waited for it to end. I would have
gotten up and gone back to my bed in the front office, but
Marjorie was enjoying herself, and I wanted to be with her.

Meanwhile, I listened as the conversation carried on,
one opinion after the next.

"I love my great-grandkids, but much of what they
do… I don't know…" one senior said, at a loss for words.
"It's strange seeing boys playing baseball on a TV screen for
hours and hours at a time, instead of going out and playing
with their friends. It doesn't make any sense to me."

"Technology has taken over these kids," another
resident replied. "Once in a while they need to turn off
everything, go outside, and breathe some fresh air."

"I must say, it sure is odd to see two people sitting
across from one another texting instead of talking," another
resident offered.

"But isn't life always changing?" Tim, the reporter,
challenged. "You can't expect the world you're born into

to be the same as the one you leave, right?"

"I love video chatting with my grandkids...who would have thought that would be possible in our lifetime?" Marjorie volunteered. "But what I fear, with all this technology, is that there will come a day when people won't interact anymore in a genuine way. That makes me sad."

"The Internet, texting, tweeting, Facebook, that's just the way it is today," I heard someone say from the back of the room. "We had our things in our time, they have theirs."

"Maybe so, but the quality of life used to be better," another senior countered. "There was less stimulus, and more time to just be. This incessant technology drives me crazy. It fills every second of every day."

"Has all of this technology made us better off?" another resident asked. "We all did just fine for a long time without it. If you ask me, a lot of it is unnecessary."

"I disagree," the senior sitting beside Marjorie said. "After being able to enlarge the type on my ereader, I couldn't go back to reading the old-fashioned way."

"I love Facebook," another voice chimed in. "It keeps me in touch with my kids and grandkids, who are all spread out."

"I'm addicted to playing Solitaire on my iPhone," a female resident offered.

"What does everyone think about TV these days?" Randi, the reporter, asked.

"It's like watching a freak show, going from one channel to the next," a male resident responded.

"Well, you must not be into watching tattoo artists compete or following the lives of mob wives," one of the female seniors kidded him.

"Boy, I have to say," Tim interjected, "it's a long way from *Leave It To Beaver* and *I Love Lucy* to shows like *Fear Factor*."

"It's unbelievable… How did we go from the greatest generation to this junk?" another asked.

"It's sad to watch the culture decline," another resident lamented. "Nowadays the idea is to do something that's shocking, vile or voyeuristic, just to get attention and make money."

"I couldn't agree more," another resident said. "It's become such a sensationalist society. What used to be indecent and outlandish is now front page news."

"Newspapers…" a male resident responded. "What a shame they're quickly becoming a thing of the past."

"There's only one thing that hasn't changed in all these years," Marjorie declared.

"What's that?" Randi asked, leaning forward with curiosity.

"He's lying at my feet," Marjorie answered, smiling and looking down at me.

"As the owner of a yellow Lab I'm crazy about, it's hard to disagree with that," Randi responded.

"Well, I think that's a good place to stop," Tim said, concluding the discussion, and then thanking the residents for their time.

When everyone started to get up, I leapt to my feet with delight. I milled around, mixing with a few of the residents, and then followed Randi and Tim back to the front office, where they chatted with Jane and Theresa for a few minutes before saying goodbye.

8

A few days after the reporters visited SunRidge, I began to sense that something wasn't right with Marjorie. At first I feared she was having a urinary tract infection, because she was agitated and restless.

Urinary tract infections are common among older people. The caregivers refer to it by its initials—UTI. But if you've ever been around an elderly person who's suffering from a UTI, you know that it should be referred to as CPS for Crazy Person Syndrome.

Marjorie contacted this insidious infection shortly after we met, and I won't soon forget it. I still remember the moment I realized something wasn't right. I was lying on her bed, when she turned to me and said, "Wrigley, can you put that donut around my neck?" Well, needless to say, there was no donut, and the only place I would have put it, if there were one, was in my mouth. I needed something to offset the agony of watching Marjorie descend into madness.

What's a dog to do, I thought, as the situation was unfolding. I stared at Marjorie's cell phone, wishing I could pick it up, and call her doctor. Instead, I got up and repositioned myself, so that I was close by Marjorie's side.

All was quiet and calm for a good while, until she pointed her finger in the air, and blurted out, "To the gallows go the dogs. Catch them all at once. I want them gone!"

At the rate things were going, gone was starting to sound real good.

Thankfully, before things got much worse, Carla came into the room and recognized our friend needed help. She didn't need to rely on her intuition or professional skills to discover there was a problem—she knew right away when Marjorie told her that, "The SunRidge spaceship had been stolen by Russian terrorists."

Carla immediately phoned Marjorie's daughter, Maureen. She arrived quickly, called a doctor, and took her mother to the hospital. Everything was taken care of, and Marjorie returned to SunRidge not long after.

The following morning when I went to visit Marjorie, her room was vacant. I tried a few hours later, and she still wasn't there. That evening, while I was eating my dinner, I overheard Jane tell Theresa that Marjorie had been taken to the hospital.

I finished eating my duck and potato kibble and rested on my bed, hoping to learn more about her condition. Soon afterward, Jane and Theresa both left the office to attend to other things. I followed Theresa around the corner to the bank of mailboxes and sat with her for a second. Then I decided to walk around the building in hopes of interacting with a couple of the residents.

It was a quiet night, and every door I passed seemed to be closed. When I went by the living room, and spotted Valerie Smith alone on the couch watching TV, I approached her. Although she was one of the residents who wasn't much of a dog person, Valerie didn't mind it when I lay at her feet, and rested my head on her slippers.

When I awoke, Valerie was gone, and I saw Theresa coming into the room to take me out for my final walk of the night.

We always took the same exit out to the courtyard, and then walked along the brick pathway, past the gazebo, to a large oak tree at the edge of the property. I liked to relieve myself on it, and Theresa enjoyed the uncluttered view of the sky from there.

The night was cool and clear, and the moon was almost a perfect circle. I watered one side of the tree, then traded places with Theresa and marked another spot—scoring a perfect bull's-eye on a splotch of bird turd.

"Beautiful moon tonight, look Wrigley," Theresa said, pointing to the sky.

I played dumb and jumped up on her, hoping she'd relinquish the treat I could smell in her left pocket, even though I knew she'd give it to me once we went back inside. She held my paws for a few seconds, before releasing me back to the ground.

"I just read the other day that the Russians sent a few dogs to the moon during the 50's and 60's. Can you imagine that?" she asked aloud, intrigued by the thought. "You'd sure look cute in one of those space suits, Wrigley. I can just see the expression on your face when the dog bones start floating through the air."

Theresa sat cross-legged on the grass, and stared out into the stillness of the night.

"Refreshment time, Wrigley," she told me, while petting my coat. "I just need five minutes of quiet with no human voices. The silence helps clear my head."

When Theresa felt better, she got up, brushed herself off, and led me back inside. Once we reached the front office, she gave me my customary nighttime treat, grabbed a few things off of her desk, leaned down to give me a hug, and then left for the evening. I curled up on my bed and waited for morning to come.

Unfortunately, I was having a hard time staying asleep. I kept getting up to scratch my bed with my paws, trying to get comfortable, but it didn't help.

Finally, I decided to leave my bed. I stretched my paws out in front of me, until my belly touched the ground, and then walked out into the hallway. It must have been around 11pm, and the place was quiet.

I wandered into the dining room, assuming the imaginary boundary line was of no consequence if the space was empty, and searched for crumbs beneath the tables. The cleaning crew must have already come through the area, because the ground was spotless.

Next, I took my usual route down Marjorie's hallway, and when I came to her room, walked through the open door. Everything looked the same as it had the day before. It felt strange to be in Marjorie's room, with all of her belongings, and not have her there. To be close to her scent, I pulled her red fleece sweatshirt off of the chair beside the armoire, with my mouth, and brought it onto the bed. I lay on top of it and quickly fell asleep.

Sometime later in the night, a couple of neighborhood cats got into a loud ruckus that shocked me out of my sleep, and brought me to my feet. I stared out the window for a while, but couldn't see anything. Before I turned to lie down again, I helped myself to a sip of stale water from a cup sitting on Marjorie's nightstand. While I was drinking, I noticed an opened box of ear plugs.

I sniffed at them, not imagining I'd have a desire to eat them. My imagination turned out to be stronger than I thought, because I ate every last one of them. To my surprise, even though ear plugs don't have much flavor, they were seriously chewy and good.

Dogs don't dwell on the consequences of their behavior, so I didn't think about the incident again. I was as surprised as Jane, when the following day she took me out to the courtyard to go potty, and I heard her yell, "EARPLUGS?! WRIGLEY, YOU'RE CRAPPING EARPLUGS!"

9

Some of the ear plugs left me through my rear end, and later, the rest left me via another orifice, to put it as pleasantly as possible.

"That's one abstract work of art," Wanda, from the cleaning crew, commented to Jane, as she surveyed the various spots on the reception area carpet, where I had left my remains.

"There's an idea for a book—vomit art," Jane said, sarcastically. "Thank God, lately he's been throwing up mostly outside."

All I could do was lie listlessly on my bed, feeling sick as, well, a dog. Sorry, I couldn't resist that one. Jane and Theresa checked on me throughout the day, becoming increasingly concerned, until they decided it was a good idea to take me to the doctor.

Vets are my least favorite people in the world. I can't think of a close second. What kind of person greets you like a friend, with enthusiasm and treats, only to poke and prod you moments later?

Unfortunately, because I've had so many different owners in my life, I've seen my fair share of them. Dr. Wolensky, the last one I went to before being adopted by the Petersons, was the best of the bunch, but I still trembled every time I got near her office.

I've been relatively healthy throughout my life, but ever since I was a puppy, I've vomited a whole lot more than the average dog. It's always the same story—eat a bunch of grass and then heave it back up along with some yellow bile or unprocessed food. Neither Dr. Wolensky, nor any of my other vets, were able to attach a name to my ongoing affliction. The process of trying to find out what was wrong, which required many vet visits through the years and several changes in my food, was far worse for me than any diagnosis could ever be. Whatever my condition was I'm sure woofing down ear plugs didn't help matters.

As we made our way that afternoon to see Dr. Sager— my current vet—Jane occasionally looked over and asked if I was okay. The look on my face plainly translated from dog to English as: *Hell no*.

When I finally got tired of nervously standing, I curled

up in the passenger seat, and listened to Van Morrison's voice, coming through the speaker near my head. He was Jane's favorite singer, and the CD seemed to be playing every time I got into her car. With the sun beaming through the front window, bathing me in warmth, I momentarily forgot where we were going.

But when the car stopped, I popped my head up, and began shaking like a naked baby in a snowstorm. Jane came around and opened the door on my side, and lured me out of the minivan. As we got near the building, I insisted on relieving myself on a well-soiled pee post that doubled as a bush by the entrance. The second I put my leg down, I pulled hard on my leash, away from the front door, but Jane was prepared for my maneuver, and spun me back around and inside the office.

The waiting room in a vet's office is a strange place. Some dogs—mostly puppies or less intelligent dogs—think they're in for a fun adventure, because they see a lot of their own kind in there. But most find out, when they get to the next room, that the experience is a far cry from a good time.

I exchanged wags and whiffs with an old Lab named Gus next to us, then retreated to a spot underneath Jane and anxiously waited. Before long, the lady behind the desk called our name, and after a quick weigh-in, we were taken to the examining room.

Jane sat down on the wooden bench, and I sat between

her legs, while we waited for the doctor to come in. Usually it took some time, which always made the wait harder to take, but on this day he came quickly.

Dr. Sager followed his standard procedure—praise, poke, prod.

"Look who we have here . . . what a good dog."

"Let's see what we have going on . . ."

"I'm just going to take a quick peek here . . ."

The vet tech, Mallory, or the decoy, as I think of them, echoed Dr. Sager's praise and promised me an after-torture treat, in an attempt to distract me from the examination.

"What's been going on with him?" Dr. Sager asked, turning to Jane.

"Well, believe it or not, he ate a bunch of earplugs."

"Believe me, I've seen worse," Dr. Sager told Jane. "Once a dog, always a child . . . right, Wrigley?"

While the two of them continued to chat, Mallory made good on her promise with a decent-sized treat by vet office standards. She then proceeded to give me a wonderfully relaxing back massage.

I was beginning to loosen up a bit, and my tail began to wag for the first time in a while. But when I looked back over at Jane and she gave me that sympathetic pout of hers, I sensed I wasn't going to like what came next.

"I'd like to keep him overnight for observation," Dr. Sager said, kneeling down and putting his hand on my head, as he delivered the blow.

57

I took the news like a dog on a leash—without a choice in the matter. Jane leaned down and squeezed me tightly, and gave me a kiss, before Mallory led me through the dreaded door to the back office.

An hour or so later, while I was half-asleep in my 3 by 2, a young woman on the veterinary staff paid me a visit, and made an innocent, yet suspicious offer.

"Wrigley, I have something super yummy and good for you," she told me, holding a syringe filled with white liquid.

It definitely didn't look like either one. So, as she moved toward me, I quickly closed my mouth.

"C'mon boy, this medicine will make you feel much better," she tried to assure me.

Well, at least she was now being honest about what it was.

"I promise it'll just take a second, Wrigley," she pleaded again. "I know you can do it."

I know I can do it too. The question is do I want to do it.

The more emphatic her voice got, the more determined I was to keep my mouth shut. After a few more failed attempts, she did what most humans do when you don't comply with their wishes—she tricked me. She parted my lips with the syringe, stuck it in a gap between my back teeth, and then squeezed the liquid into my mouth, forcing me to swallow.

Ick, double ick!

The evening wasn't much better. The dog next to me, a large one whose breed I couldn't tell, made a loud wheezing noise throughout the night. The poor guy was so uncomfortable and agitated in that small, cold, metal cage, I don't think he slept a wink.

Thankfully, my stay was only for one night. The next morning, when Jane came to pick me up, my tail was wagging so hard, it could have knocked over a small child.

10

When I returned to SunRidge, Veronica greeted me with a welcome home present that smelled from here to eternity—a smoked rawhide braid. Jane didn't look too happy about her giving me a treat so soon after returning from the vet, but once you show it to the dog, you owe it to the dog. I wasted no time in bringing the prize to my bed, and digging in.

After making a decent dent on one of the corners of my gift, I got up to take a walk around, so I could socialize with the residents, and see if Marjorie had returned.

Soon after I left the front office, I got diverted, when my nose picked up some interesting odors coming from the laundry room. During the daytime hours, May Clayfield was on staff, and she always allowed me to indulge in one of my canine fetishes—smelling dirty clothes.

When I walked inside the room, there was a large pile of clothes on the ground in front of one of the washers. May was folding laundry across the way with her back to me, so I began snooping through the mound. While my nose was buried in a woman's blouse, I heard a gasp.

"Oh my God! What are you doing here?" a stranger's voice shrieked. "You just about gave me a heart attack."

The woman, who I thought was May, turned out to be a new employee. She walked over and knelt down beside me.

"May didn't tell me anything about a dog when she trained me," the woman said. "But you seem like a sweet— let me check—boy."

I looked at her name tag, which read Vicki. Her breath smelled of hamburger meat—my favorite—so I licked her mouth. She smiled and gave me a long stroke from my head to my tail.

To be on the safe side, Vicki decided to bring me up to the front office. After Theresa told her it was okay for me to be out and about, I followed her back to the laundry room, before continuing down the hallway toward Marjorie's room.

As I got closer, I could feel my heart begin to beat faster. Her door was open, but again, no one was inside. I sniffed and looked around for any new clues about her

61

condition, but didn't find any. Although I was sad that Marjorie wasn't there, seeing her things untouched made me hopeful that she was coming back. It was just a matter of time.

When I left the room to continue making my rounds, I crossed paths with Walter. He glanced over at me and grunted, before heading down the hallway in the opposite direction.

When I passed by the library, I saw a handful of Marjorie's friends gathered together for their knitting group. Virginia Woodson, Marjorie's best friend at Sun-Ridge, spotted me standing in the hall and called me to her.

"Come and keep us company, Wrigley," she said, happy to see me. "We could use a dog's love right about now."

I greeted each of the ladies, soaking up their warm reception, and sniffing at their yarn and knitting needles. With all of the different colored bundles of fuzzy string they had gathered around them, this group would be a cat's meow.

After I found a spot on the floor to lie, I listened while the women talked about the new patterns and yarns they were excited about. However, it didn't take long for Marjorie's name to come up in the conversation.

"Oh, I hope she gets better soon," Betty Severson said, holding her hand over her heart. "I called my pastor this morning and we prayed together for her. This place just wouldn't be the same without Marjorie."

"Think positive, Betty… I think everything's going to be all right," Bernice Carmichael offered. "Next week this time, she'll be sitting right here with us, telling us some funny story about her hospital stay."

"From your lips to God's ears," Betty replied. "I just worry about Marjorie…she has so many health complications."

"Don't we all," Bernice responded.

"Thank God for knitting," Joyce Brower said, changing the subject. "It's great therapy for times like these."

"Joyce, can you believe I've been knitting since I was seven years old?" Virginia asked.

"How'd you start?" Joyce asked.

"My mother was a Girl Scout leader. She was teaching my older sister and the other girls, and I wanted to learn."

"My husband used to give me a hard time, because I couldn't watch television without knitting," Betty interjected.

"I didn't know there was any other way to watch TV," Bernice responded with a laugh.

"I used to love knitting sweaters," Joan Tartunian shared with the group, "but with this darn arthritis, now I stick to socks and smaller stuff."

"Nobody tell Wrigley," Virginia said in a hushed voice, "but I'm going to make him something really special."

I popped up at the mention of my name, and put my head on Virginia's lap.

"Look at him … now he's curious," Joan said, laughing.

"Did you understand what I was saying?" Virginia asked me, while petting my head, "Well, you'll just have to wait to see what it is."

The tranquility of five women knitting was suddenly interrupted by the enthusiasm of two energetic kids, when a family friend of Marjorie's, who didn't know she was in the hospital, dropped off her teenagers for a visit.

The ladies were at a loss as to how to handle the situation, and there was an awkward feeling in the room. Luckily, Jane came by and took the teenagers, Griffin and Skylar, out to the courtyard.

When they returned, having learned where Marjorie was, the children were sad and subdued. Knowing that kids and dogs go together like peanut butter and chocolate, Jane suggested, "Why don't you guys take Wrigley down to the park."

I looked up at everyone, excited and ready to go.

Most of my walks were around the grounds of Sun-Ridge, or if Jane or Theresa were up for a longer one, we'd go around the neighboring streets. So Bennett Park, a few blocks away, was a nice treat.

The place I wished we could visit more often was the dog park. Every time we went there, I had so much fun. Unfortunately, it was a decent distance from SunRidge, and time was in short supply for a working family, like the Petersons.

When we arrived at the park, the kids let me off the leash, and I ran around with a rambunctious brown dog named Leroy. I had met him once before on one of my walks with Theresa or Jane; I can't remember which.

On that occasion, Leroy was much more likable, because he was on a leash. This time, he had an annoying, insatiable desire to hump me. Whenever I got close, he glommed on to my backside and wouldn't let go.

His owner, a man in his 50's, wearing a tie-dyed t-shirt, didn't seem to notice or care. He was too busy singing this song—*He's glad, glad Leroy Brown, happiest dog in the whole damn town, romping and running all around, free from that God-awful pound*—over and over again, in a horribly bad voice.

After Leroy and his owner left, the kids and I played a great game of hide and seek. They scurried off and hid behind large trees and trash cans, and then called my name. When I found them, they rewarded me with a liver treat from a small baggie Jane gave them before we left.

As we were heading back to SunRidge, the youngest kid (they always have the best ideas), Griffin suggested an alternate plan. First, we'd go across the street and get a soft serve ice-cream, and then we'd return.

The kids ordered a small cup of vanilla for me, and put it on one of the outdoor benches where we sat. I excitedly licked away, finishing before anyone. Skylar, sensing I was still not satisfied, gave me the last piece of her cone.

65

Once we returned, and the kids said goodbye to Jane, I went back to the front office and lay on my bed. Before I fell asleep, I thought about Marjorie. Why was it taking so long for her to come back? Was she getting better? Did she miss my company?

11

The following morning, after I finished my breakfast, I walked out of the front office and saw Marjorie's daughter, Maureen, coming in alone through the sliding glass entrance. The sorrow and heaviness on her face told me that Marjorie was in very bad shape, or had passed away. Sensing her mood, I gave her a subtle greeting before walking by her side to her mother's room.

While Maureen slowly wandered around the living room, touching and holding some of Marjorie's things, I lay down on the kitchen floor. When she went into the bedroom, I waited a few moments before joining her, and found a spot beside the armoire. I watched as she made a loop around the room, and then sat down on the side of her mother's bed.

For a long while, Maureen just sat there, staring at the floor, lost in thought. Then, she looked over and seemed to notice me for the first time. She softly patted the bed for me to come to her. I walked over, sat by her feet, and looked up.

"My mother loved you so much, Wrigley," she told me, her eyes swollen and red. "Thank you for comforting her the way you did." She stopped talking for a few moments and rubbed the side of my face before continuing. "I thought for sure I'd have her for a few more years, but God has his reasons. She's with my father now."

There are times I've wished dogs could speak, but this was not one of them. I knew there was nothing I could say to make the moment easier for Marjorie's daughter. So I leaned my head against her knee, while she ran her hand through my coat, and cried.

I had been with family members in these situations before, and felt their unbearable grief and loss. Time—the best remedy—took time, and that was a long way off. My job was to be a bridge of comfort for as long as they needed me.

"She was the best mother I could have ever wished for," Maureen told me, dabbing her tears with a tissue, "but we didn't start out close."

I backed away from her, jumped on the bed, and rested on my side. She followed my lead, and fell back on the bed, lying beside me with her head propped on a pillow.

"I was jealous that she belonged to the world as much as she belonged to me," she went on. "But I grew to understand that she was an angel, and angels always have people around them."

Maureen stopped talking for a moment and stared at a large photograph of her mother and father on the wall. The picture showed Marjorie and Frank in their later years, arm in arm at the beach with happy grins on their faces. "They were quite a pair," she said with a smile. "It's hard to find love that lasts that long for the right reasons. They had their differences, like any couple, but as my mother often told me, they vowed to never go to bed angry at one another." Maureen turned her head and looked back toward me. "I was blessed to have two incredible parents. They were nurturing, loving, and supportive, and when the time came, they let me fly from the nest to make my way in the world. Roots and wings, a child can't ask for anything more."

Maureen grew quiet and teary-eyed again, so I leaned over and gave her hand the warm tongue treatment, licking it over and over again. When I finished, I turned and rolled onto my back. We were both staring at the ceiling now, which struck Maureen as funny, and she burst out laughing.

"Only a dog could make me laugh at a time like this," she said, leaning over to rub my belly.

After a few more minutes, Maureen got up and gathered a few of her mother's belongings, and walked back to the front office. She gave Jane and Theresa long hugs goodbye, and then reached down, cradled my head in her hands, and kissed my forehead before leaving.

A couple of days later, I watched sadly as movers paraded past the front office, taking away everything from Marjorie's room. I knew it would only be a matter of time before another resident would occupy her space. Life goes on. But a person you love becomes a part of you, and it's hard to imagine life without them.

You'd think being a dog with a short life compared to a human, and living at an assisted living home, I'd have some great wisdom on death. I wish I did. I know one day I'll comfort my last resident, chase my last ball, and taste my last treat. It happens to all of us. We reach the end of the line. I suppose life is about what you do before that time comes.

Judging from the love Marjorie's daughter, friends, and I had for her, she had done quite a lot.

12

Marjorie was special. Everyone at SunRidge was sad, and we all did our best to move through the sorrow and carry on.

The Petersons knew that I was closer to Marjorie than I was to any other resident, and that many people at Sun-Ridge referred to me as *her* dog. They went out of their way to keep my spirits up.

Jane let me run free in the courtyard more often than usual, Tamara took me on walks around SunRidge during her lunch break; Ron took me to the dog park one week-end afternoon, and Veronica—knowing my obsession for stuffed animals—gave me a cute, fleece pig, who squealed for mercy, but I didn't show it any.

It all helped, but I still felt best sitting inside the doorway of Marjorie's now vacant room, thinking that at any moment I'd smell her scent, or see her slowly coming down the hallway behind her walker, smiling.

No such miracle occurred.

Instead, one day, while I was sitting in my spot, a Cavalier King Charles Spaniel puppy came wiggling down the hallway, with a human companion. The dog couldn't have been more than a few months old, and she had a pink bow tied above her ear. She was still in that puppy stage when your body wobbles like Jell-O, and it's hard to concentrate on anything for long.

As she approached me, I stood up and sniffed her from behind and then below. When her companion gently pulled on her leash to continue walking, I followed her irresistible scent to the living room, where a group of seniors were gathered.

The puppy's human companion took her one by one to visit with the seniors, lifting her onto their laps. The residents showered her with kisses, scratches, and treats. It was a love fest, and for the first time in a long time, the attention at SunRidge was being directed at a dog other than me.

"Oh my, she's beautiful," one resident gushed.

"What's her name?" another resident asked.

"This is Daphne," her human companion answered.

"She'd sure make someone a fine dog," someone else

added.

"Can you put her on my lap, please?" a resident requested.

"She's so sweet … soft too," another one commented.

You often hear people singing the praises of dogs—we're smart, selfless, loyal, and the list goes on. But nothing in life is perfect, except for things you can eat or chew. Dogs can be super-jealous. I'm living proof.

As the puppy continued to be passed around, I sniffed at her, and tried to nose my way between her and the residents, hoping to intercept some of the attention she was getting. My efforts were useless—everyone was totally smitten with the puppy.

Watching the residents respond to Daphne reminded me of my days at the shelter, when humans would go gaga whenever a puppy was up for adoption. I always thought it was short-sighted to fall in love with something that's not going to stay that way for very long. At least with a grown or older dog, you know what you're getting. But maybe that was just sour grapes, because I was being passed over for younger pups.

Okay, fine, let them fawn over you, Daphne, and then be gone, I thought to myself, as I withdrew and lay down nearby.

Aside from my jealousy, I had an important, unanswered question—*Is this a regular occurrence or a one-time mistake?*

Thankfully, it turned out that the puppy belonged to one of the residents' great-grandchildren, and she thought the seniors would enjoy meeting the dog.

I was already sad about losing Marjorie, and seeing the residents doting on another dog didn't help my spirits.

Later that day, camped out again inside of Marjorie's doorway, even someone as insensitive as Walter seemed to notice I wasn't my usual spunky self. After coming out of his room to complain about the noise the cleaning crew was making, while they prepared Marjorie's room for the next resident, he actually spoke to me.

"I know you liked the old lady, but that's life. You're born and you die, and the truth is there's not much in-between but struggle and strife," he said, before walking back to his room.

I was shocked when he returned moments later, holding a box of peanut butter biscuits—the ones Marjorie kept on her kitchen counter.

"I grabbed these from her room, before they took everything away. You want one?" he asked me, holding a biscuit in his hand.

Of course, I did. They were my favorites. But I wanted to show Walter that it would take more than food to win my friendship. So I gently took the biscuit from his hand, and then let it drop from my mouth.

If anyone tells you that there isn't a high price to pay in the name of pride, they're lying.

Walter didn't show any reaction to my rejection of his offer. He slowly walked over and kicked the treat a couple of times, until it was inside of his room, and closed the door.

Before long, Marjorie's room was clean, with new carpet and a fresh coat of paint. No matter how hard I tried, I could no longer detect even the faintest aroma of her scent.

A week or so later, a lady named Ellen Lubuck, who had a cat named Jerry, who didn't like a dog named Wrigley, moved into Marjorie's room. Jane caught me a few times, lying a little ways down from Ellen's door, trying to hang on to the past. Each time she brought me back to the front office.

Perhaps Jerry was a blessing in disguise, because even if Ellen had wanted my company, in my heart that space would always be reserved for Marjorie.

During this time of transition, I remembered one of Marjorie's favorite sayings—*Our days are numbered, all we can do is treasure our time*.

How true, I thought, looking back and cherishing all of the ordinary, quiet times that she and I spent together. With her gone, they now seemed even more special.

On one of those lazy days, when Marjorie wasn't feeling particularly well, she told me that after she passed away and got to heaven, she would send me a sign to let me know she had arrived. I wondered what it would be, and when it might happen.

13

On a quiet Sunday afternoon the following week, I encountered Walter again in an unusual way. It was the time of day when the last football game had ended, and dinner hadn't come yet. I was hungry and bored, just wandering around in search of a snack to tide me over, or a guest to be with.

Every resident I normally visited had their doors closed, and the staff members were too busy to give me any attention. I was going to head back to the front office, but out of habit, I turned and began walking toward Marjorie's old room. When I got near to what Carla used to call the intersection of joy and pain—in reference to her association with Marjorie and Walter—I heard classical music coming from Walter's room.

His door was open, and I curiously poked my head inside. I was astounded by what I saw. Walter was sitting in his recliner, his head tilted back and his eyes closed, taking in the music like it was a symphony composed to save his soul. He looked like the sweetest man you'd ever seen.

The music was loud enough so that he didn't hear me enter the room. I sniffed around his kitchen, coming up with a couple of small pieces of cheddar cheese, and some bread crumbs.

When I looked back up at Walter, he was still in complete bliss. Humans are definitely more complicated than dogs, I thought to myself. Could it be possible that Walter, like many hard things, was actually soft on the inside?

I guess I was about to find out.

When Walter opened his eyes—a few seconds after the piece of music ended—I was sitting in front of him like a well-behaved school boy, waiting for the teacher to arrive. He slowly moved his head from one side to the other, before lowering his gaze and spotting me. He was startled, but not visibly upset. He didn't move, and neither did I. We just looked at one another for a moment, taking each other's measure.

Then, he broke the silence.

"This isn't a good idea, you being in my room," he said, pushing himself off of the recliner to get up.

I feared the effect of the music was wearing off.

Bach, Beethoven, Mozart, someone begin to play!

"Come on, out you go," he said, pointing toward the door.

I was on my way when I spotted one of his socks, rolled up in a ball near the couch. I spontaneously ran over, picked it up with my mouth, and dropped it at his feet, hoping, like a crazy fool, for a game of fetch.

"No fetch. Get!" he demanded, motioning again for me to leave.

When I hesitated for a second, he grabbed one of Marjorie's peanut butter biscuits from the kitchen counter. He used it to lure me out into the hallway. Just before he closed the door, I looked up at him, as if to say: *I'm ready for my treat now.* Either Walter didn't understand dog very well, or he forgot to give me the treat, because he closed the door in my face.

14

After Marjorie died, I spent more time in the front office with Jane and Theresa than I had in a long while. They gave me love and attention as they always had, getting up from behind their desks, if they noticed me rolled on my back with my paws in the air, hoping for a belly rub, or sensed I could use a new chewbone or toy.

But Jane and Theresa were extremely busy running SunRidge, not to mention managing their own private lives.

Sometimes, I'd sit on my bed with my head cradled between my paws, and just watch the two of them. Their days were filled with phone calls, interviews, tours, troubleshooting, and paperwork. It never seemed to end. From a dog's perspective, human life is filled with too much work, and not enough play. When God created people, he forgot to include one thing—a button you could press to get them to stop everything. I could sure use it some days, just to get Jane and Theresa to leave their work behind, and run delirious circles of joy with me in the courtyard and feel free as a dog.

Delivery people coming to SunRidge always broke up the monotony of work a bit. Jane and Theresa were friendly with many of them, and they often popped into the front office for a quick hello.

My favorite of them all was Gary, the UPS driver. It could rain for a month straight without a sliver of sunshine, and Gary would still have a smile on his face. Luckily for me, he loved dogs, and had a few himself. I always followed Gary right to the door when he left, sad to see him go. Sometimes he'd turn back and wave.

Dogs live for fresh scents and new adventures, so I was super-excited when on one visit, Gary asked Jane if he could take me out to this truck.

"I want to get a picture of all the dogs on my route, sitting in the driver's seat of my truck," he told her.

Jane happily obliged, leading me out to the big brown truck, and then unleashing me. I excitedly hopped aboard and sniffed around the front cab area, until Gary climbed into the driver's seat and called me to him. He handed his phone to Jane through the window, and then huddled close beside me, while she took our picture.

In time, I began to venture out of the front office as often as I had before Marjorie passed away. A few days earlier in the library after lunchtime, I met a friendly new resident named John Stokely. He wore a fedora hat that looked and smelled as if it had been around the world.

I decided to go by the library again to see if he was there. Sure enough, John was sitting in the same spot, wearing his trusty hat, and reading a book. Humans, just like dogs, are creatures of habit.

John was happy to look up from *Flowers for Algernon*, and see me standing in front of him.

"Well, if it isn't my new friend. Hello again," he said, with a smile.

I sat down, and then lifted my paw for a shake.

He put down his book, and accepted my offer.

"A polite dog, someone must have taught you good manners."

I reached over and sniffed the spine of his book, and licked the cover a couple of times.

"Well-educated too . . . I didn't know dogs could read," he said, with a chuckle.

When John went back to his book, I curled up a few feet away, and went to sleep. I soon found myself far off in a dream.

Marjorie and I are walking along a winding path that is surrounded by rolling green hills, covered with wildflowers. It's spring—her favorite season—and the air is fragrant and alive. In the distance, the mountain caps are still covered with snow. After we've traveled a ways, she leans down and unclips my leash, so I can sniff and mark everything around me, and swim in the nearby stream.

When I finally rejoin her, she tells me to sit and wait, while she continues alone down the path. When she gets about twenty yards away, a strange thing begins to happen. The further down the path she travels, the younger she looks. At first the difference is subtle, but gradually she begins to appear younger and younger. When Marjorie has become a little girl, she stops, turns towards me, smiles, waves, and then disappears.

At that point, my body twitched hard, and I woke up. After I got to my feet, and gave myself a good shake, I realized that John had left the library. I followed his scent to a room at the end of the corridor.

The door was open, so I entered.

"Boy, you sure are a smart one," he said, impressed with my tracking skills.

John was sitting on a large recliner at the other end of the room. I walked over and sat beside him.

"Your spirit reminds me of an old dog of mine...Jake," he told me, petting my head gently. "He was a mix of Lab and something else. Smart as a whip, and loyal and loving as the day is long."

While John launched into a long story about Jake, I looked around his place. There was something everywhere—papers piled high on his coffee table; stacks of magazines and newspapers on the floor beside the TV stand; clothes draped over his couch; and an oxygen tank, along with another medical device, close to his recliner.

The walls were covered with many photographs from his life. There was young John, old young, and everything in-between. An old dog looks differently than it did as a puppy, but the change in a person's appearance over the span of their life can be dramatic. In John's case, time had been kind to him, and you could still see some of the young boy in the old man's face.

When John stopped talking to me, I found a spot nearby and made myself comfortable. The TV was on, so I glanced at the screen. Golf… I watched for a few seconds, and then began scanning the photographs above the TV. One, toward the top of the wall, instantly grabbed my attention. It showed John dressed in a white coat with a large dog standing on a table beside him.

Oh no, John was a vet!

The picture looked to be many years old, and I assumed by now he had retired from his old, invasive ways. Can you imagine though, if out of the blue, he turned to me and said, "Wrigley, I need you to turn on your side for me?"

After a while, John got up to open the blinds. I followed him to the window, put my head on the sill, and stared out. Across the street, there was a young boy throwing a baseball with his father on one of the baseball diamonds in the park.

Once John returned to his recliner, he picked up on my view. "You can't beat that . . . grass beneath your feet, blue skies above you, fresh air, and the pop of the mitt," he said. "It sure brings back memories of my son, Alan. That was his sport. He was a stand-out second baseman in high school, and broke most of the school's records for hitting. He had several scholarship offers to play college ball…"

John's voice trailed off, and he stopped talking.

I turned away from the window, sniffed at a medicine bottle on the edge of the coffee table, and settled back in the same spot as before. When I glanced over at John his eyes were teary.

"Now that I'm an old man, I can say that it's true . . . you never get over losing a child. It's not the way it's supposed to be, you know," he said, looking back out the window. "Some days it feels as fresh as yesterday, when I lost my boy to cancer. He was my only child, and the heartbreak and sadness of losing him eventually broke his mother and I apart."

John took off his glasses, and wiped away the tears coming down his face with a handkerchief. Afterward, he stared down at his glasses and the handkerchief on his lap, for a long while, before he began to speak again.

"I'm not the type of person that looks back and regrets

things," he said, "but I wish I hadn't worked so hard when Alan was growing up. I always thought I'd make up for it somewhere down the line, but I learned the hard way that tomorrow is for fools and dreamers. Now is all we have."

John reached over to the end table beside him, and took a sip of cranberry juice. Then, he looked over at me.

"Shortly after Alan died is when I got Jake. A friend brought him to me, and I thought it was a crazy idea. What was I going to do with a dog in my condition? But it turned out to be what Jake could do for me. He comforted me as well as anyone could at the time. From the moment I got that dog he wouldn't leave my side, day or night. When I cried, he would come over and drape his paws on me. When I opened my eyes every morning, he somehow managed to stir the little life left in me to get me out of the house. We took long walks together through the woods. That dog healed me…"

John winced and swallowed hard, holding back another flood of emotions. Then, a smile came across his face. "A few years later, Wrigley, I remarried and had another son. Guess what I named him? You guessed it . . . Jake."

After John talked for a little while longer, I looked over and he was asleep. When I got up to change the position I was lying in, he opened his eyes.

"Okay, I suppose it's time for you to get going," he said, stretching his arms into the air. "I've got a few things to do before my card game."

Using the arms of his walker, John lifted himself up, and then slowly walked toward the door. When he reached me, I was waiting patiently in the kitchen. I glanced up at the counter, my ritual before leaving any resident's room, in hopes that John could send me on my way with something good to eat. He smiled at my suggestion, opened the refrigerator, reached into a bag of carrots and tossed one out into the hallway. I happily scrambled for it and crunched on it, while the door closed behind me.

Visits like this were not uncommon for me. Many of the seniors at SunRidge had unresolved issues, regrets, or deep hurts in their lives. And who better to share them with than the house dog?

15

The holiday season is a complicated mix of excitement and angst. I can always feel it in the air as it gets closer. Routines and schedules begin to fall away, and are replaced by a frenzy of activity and festivities.

It's always been my favorite time of the year, because it's the only time of the year when humans collectively match the spirit of dogs. There is so much joy and love and good cheer everywhere.

Unfortunately, it can be a lonely and difficult time for many of the residents at SunRidge. Some are distant from their family members, either geographically or in their connection to them; others feel the sadness of spending the holidays without a lifelong spouse, who recently passed away. As a result, during the holidays is often when I am needed the most.

Thanksgiving arrived as it always did—with delicious smells wafting from the kitchen. The SunRidge chefs always created an incredible turkey dinner for the residents, of which about half stayed for the occasion. The others would leave to spend it with family or friends.

Regrettably, Jane and Ron deemed the Thanksgiving meal too formal for the house dog to attend or even to be around. Ron, in particular, felt it wasn't a good idea for guests of the residents, who were visiting SunRidge, to have a dog eagerly staring at them while they enjoyed their turkey with all of the trimmings. I suppose it made sense, but to ban me from at least watching the biggest food feast of the year seemed unfair.

Jane would always put me in what she called a "stay and chill" on my bed, when the Thanksgiving meal was about to be served. Sometime later, she would return with leftovers for me to enjoy.

It was hard to feel bad about being kept in the front office for special holiday meals, in light of how few rules the Petersons imposed on me. However, there are occasions when too much is stirring for a dog to be still, and Thanksgiving, for me, was always one of them.

I lay on my bed for what seemed like a good while, before getting up and sniffing around Theresa's desk. She often ate lunch there, and would accidently drop pieces of her sandwich on the floor. I didn't come up with anything.

After another long period of restlessness and boredom, listening to far off voices coming from the dining room, I did something highly unusual for me—I broke Jane's command, and wandered out of the office.

The first person I crossed paths with was Pedro, the SunRidge handyman, who didn't know I wasn't supposed to be walking around.

"Hey there, Wrigley ... how goes it?" he asked me, after taking a seat on a chair in front of one of the resident's rooms.

He gave me a scratch beneath my chin, and then leaned forward and rested his head in his hands. I slipped between his forearms and gave him a lick on the nose. He laughed, and then wiped my saliva off with a towel he had on his shoulder.

"Well, I guess someone's gotta work on Thanksgiving," he said, leaning back in the chair. "I can't wait to get out of here and be with my family."

When Pedro got up and walked away, I stopped in the doorway of the next room I came to, which was Sandi Schifman's. Something drew me inside, and when I entered the empty room, I immediately spotted it. On Sandi's bed there was an old teddy bear propped up against the bed frame. It was the first time I had ever seen him, and he struck me as the kind of bear that would taste much better than he looked.

Thoughts of tearing apart the decrepit old fella danced in my head.

I hoped onto the bed, sniffed around the bear, and then took him down to the ground. I began to gnaw on one of his arms, when I suddenly remembered the reprimand I received after destroying Lola Gladlock's friend, Foster the elephant. I licked the old bear's nose a couple of times, and then decided to let him be.

I left Sandi's room and continued down the hallway. Some of the doors were open, but most of them were closed. I stopped and sniffed at a few of the ones which were festively decorated for the holidays, in most cases, by the residents' children and grandchildren. For each holiday throughout the year, SunRidge had a competition for the most creatively decorated door. The winner got bragging rights and a gift card from a store of their choice.

When I got to Walter's room, I had every intention of walking by without stopping, but I smelled turkey through the tiny crack in his door.

I veered over slowly, and gently inserted my snout in the crack, until I could fit my head inside. Walter was fast asleep on the couch, sitting upright, and snoring loudly. His neck was tilted to one side, and his breathing sounded like an old train, struggling to move down the tracks.

Standing in the kitchen, I wondered if I should turn and leave, remembering how my last visit ended with Walter showing me the door, or if I should stay and see, if there was indeed, a turkey dinner for the house dog.

Before I could thoroughly weigh my options, I found myself at the edge of Walter's coffee table, in striking distance of his Thanksgiving feast! From where I was, I could see his plate—it was filled with a large portion of turkey, mashed potatoes smothered in gravy, yams, string beans, and a small pile of cranberry sauce. It looked as though Walter had taken a few bites, and then fallen asleep.

My nose was dancing with delight—I couldn't turn back now. I lunged over and started scarfing down the food on Walter's plate faster than Yogi Bear and Boo Boo ever stole a picnic basket.

I inhaled the white and dark meat on his plate first, and then licked clean the mashed potatoes. Next, I worked on the yams and the string beans. I finished by having a few bites of the cranberry sauce.

When I was through, I looked up, and Walter was still snoring up a storm.

It's hard to say exactly what happened next. I remember walking around Walter's place for a little while, and then beginning to feel incredibly sleepy.

The next thing I heard was a man's voice. When I opened my eyes, I realized I had fallen asleep on the couch, with my head against Walter's leg!

"You little devil you. What are you doing in my room?" he asked, startled.

I quickly sprang up and snapped out of my slumber.

The other shoe was about to drop.

"You ate my turkey dinner!" Walter cried out in disbelief.

Who me? You may not know this about dogs, Walter, but we have extremely poor memories. I have no recollection of what happened before I fell asleep. Therefore, I'm innocent of any wrongdoing. Oddly though, I can remember the exact spot where I discovered the tasty remains of a rodent on a walk I took three weeks ago with Jane. It sure is nice being a dog sometimes.

I got down from the couch and looked at Walter, as if to say: *I plead the fifth.* He picked up the plate and took it to the kitchen. When he turned back toward the living room and met my gaze, he seemed less angry. Begrudgingly, I think he was beginning to develop an admiration for my dogged determination.

Walter didn't have to kick me out this time. I left on my own accord, returning to the front office before Jane noticed I was gone.

16

Not long after Thanksgiving, one evening after I finished my dinner, I got a surprise.

I suppose it wasn't a complete surprise. A dog always knows by observing human behavior, when something out of the ordinary is about to happen. In this case, Theresa kept trying to distract me from seeing what Jane was doing in the corner of the room a few hours earlier, and the two of them, along with Veronica, seemed a bit more giddy than usual.

So I knew something was brewing, I just didn't know what it was, or when it would happen.

I didn't have to wait long. I was lying in the reception area when Carla, Ron Peterson, Tamara Peterson, and a few of the residents, came walking toward me. Someone turned out the lights, and I heard Veronica yell, "Happy Birthday, Wrigley!" A cheer went up, as the lights came back on.

In my excitement, I jumped up on Jane, who was the closest to me. She held my front paws for a few seconds, dancing back and forth before releasing me. Ron reached over and gave me one of his rousing "atta boy" body pats. Veronica blew out the candles on the cake she was holding, and then pulled each one out before handing it to Jane. She and I posed with the cake, while Ron took our picture.

Before I could dig in, Jane read the inscription aloud, "Happy Birthday to our loyal and loving house dog, Wrigley!" Everyone clapped and cheered again.

I showed my appreciation by sticking my snout in the center of the small, round vanilla cake, and took a large chunk out of it. After a few more bites, Ron gave me a gift to unwrap. I excitedly tore at the paper, and uncovered a gift basket filled with treats. He let me grab one of the larger biscuits before lifting the basket off of the ground, and putting it away.

The next gift wasn't edible, so Jane unwrapped it for me.

"How thoughtful … Maureen, on behalf of Marjorie, got him these," Jane said, holding up DVD's from the National Geographic show, *Dogtown*.

The mention of Marjorie's name brought a sense of sadness over the group. Everyone—me included—still missed her very much.

"How old is he now?" Sandi Schifman asked, coming over to say hello to me.

"Eight," Theresa answered.

"With this sweet boy though," Jane said, getting down on her knees to wrap her arms around me, "we don't count years . . . we count our blessings every day that he's in our lives, and here to comfort the residents."

"That's so sweet, Mom," Tamara responded.

"You can see who the most loved and pampered male in our family is," Ron joked.

"Well, he's my only son," Jane beamed, still hugging me.

"But I'm your only husband," Ron responded. "At least that I know of."

"Oh, come on, honey, don't be jealous," Jane replied.

While Ron and Jane continued to banter back and forth, Sandi Schifman leaned over the side of her wheelchair to pat my head. "Wrigley, you're a senior citizen now, just like the rest of us," she told me. "I'm starting to see some grey in your muzzle."

"That's right, in dog years he's eligible to be a member of AARP, or as I like to call it—AAR, I can barely Pee," John Stokely joked, referencing the male anatomy that slows with age.

I suppose the residents were right—taking into account my age and size, I would probably be considered an older dog. But dogs age differently than humans. Our final years are brief, and in most cases, we don't suffer from long illnesses. We pretty much go until we're gone. I think I prefer it that way.

Over the past couple of months, I did notice a few signs of aging beginning to creep in. It took me a bit longer to chase down a ball, and I could feel some aches and pains before I got going in the morning. I just didn't pay any attention to them. A dog's life is short, and you have to soak up every bit of it while you can, ailments be damned.

The only things I feared about getting older were not being able to smell and taste as well. And of course, enduring more of those awful excursions to Dr. Sager's office.

17

The time between Christmas and New Year's is normally quiet and uneventful, but a watershed moment—the kind that separates everything that came before it, and everything that comes after—was about to occur at SunRidge. It was so out of the ordinary for anything I'd ever experienced as the house dog, it still feels surreal recounting the details.

I was sound asleep on my bed in the front office after Jane, Theresa, and most the staff had gone home for the evening, when something caused me to awaken. I walked out into the hallway to see what it might have been. When I looked down both of the corridors, they were empty, and nothing looked unusual.

As I turned to go back to the front office, I heard movement. I looked up and spotted someone at the far end of one of the corridors. I couldn't make out who it was, but I could tell from the shape of the figure that it was a female. For a split second, I thought it might have been Linda, the overnight caregiver on duty, but she was slighter and smaller than whoever this was.

Instinctively, I began heading down the hallway toward the person. When she heard the sound of my collar jangling, she looked startled. She froze for a second, and then began walking toward me at a quick pace.

As the person got closer, I realized it was Corina, one of Walter's caregivers. When our paths met in the middle of the hallway, she was sweating and seemed scattered.

"Let's go, dog, let's go," she told me hurriedly, leading me back toward the front office. I anxiously spun around and followed her. When we turned the corner, she shooed me into the office, closed the door behind her, and walked away.

I stood by the door for a few moments, wondering what to make of the situation. The rage I saw in Corina's eyes reminded me of Norm, when he would get angry at me, but far more intense.

My mind flashed on the times he would lock me in the garage, when Tracie would leave the house. Eventually, I learned how to open the side door by clawing at the handle with my front paws until it turned. Then I would let myself

18

The next morning I drove back to SunRidge with Theresa. Although Jane and Ron had spent the night there, trying to calm down the residents, you could still feel the tension, as soon as we walked through the front door.

Theresa unclipped me from my leash, and I made a loop around the building to see if I could lighten up the somber mood. I found many of the residents scattered in small groups, talking about the incident, and still noticeably shaken.

A happy dog with a wagging tail, and a wet nose, was definitely a welcomed sight. As each of them interacted with me, and slowly pet my coat, their breathing became more relaxed. In their conversations, the residents wondered aloud what the fallout would be from the previous night.

Would Walter sue the Petersons and Corina? Would he return to SunRidge? If so, in what condition? What would happen to Corina? Would she go to jail?

It would take a while for their questions to be answered, but at the moment, it seemed hard for anyone to believe that life at SunRidge would ever be the same again.

But even as everyone was pondering what the future might hold, life was slowly returning to normal. Carla was making the rounds, comforting the residents with her warm ways. Sandi Schifman, along with a few other residents, was going to a stretching class. Ethel Leeds and Harriet Tobin were having tea in the library. I was giving greeting sniffs to a new resident named Karen Kratzer, who was showing Veronica pictures of her first great-grandchild. And Jane and Theresa were at their desks, working away.

Although life went on, the incident was still the topic of most conversations for the next couple of days. Some residents felt that Walter got what he deserved.

"I'm sorry, but what goes around, comes around," I overheard Virginia Greer say over lunch, in earshot of the dining room boundary line, where I was resting.

"If you ask me," Dee Dildyne offered, sitting next to Virginia, "he's an arrogant you know what."

"But to be abused like that … horrible," Joan Hardwick responded.

"I agree, Joan," Claudine Merrit said. "Nobody deserves to be viciously attacked under any circumstances."

Jane and Theresa discussed the incident as well in the front office.

"Don't get me wrong—what Corina did was unconscionable," Theresa told her mother, later that afternoon. "But I don't think she's a bad person. She just snapped. I wish she would have quit before she got to that point."

"That's ridiculous!" Jane quickly responded, while waiting on hold with the hospital to check on Walter's condition. "Everyone gets angry, but you have to be evil to get in a rage and hurt someone like that. Especially an old man."

Another day passed, and just as the awful incident was beginning to fade from everyone's consciousness, Walter returned to SunRidge. He looked very different than he had on the first day he arrived. This time, he had a large bandage across his forehead, his arm was in a sling, and he had a subdued expression on his face.

My first instinct was to go over to him and say hello, but I thought better of it, and decided instead to lie down in front of the reception area couch, while he talked with Veronica. When he finished telling her about his ordeal at the hospital, he looked back at me and said, "And I wouldn't be here, if it weren't for Wrigley."

It was the first time Walter ever called me by my name. I got up and walked over to his scooter, and sniffed around it, taking in where he'd been. When I sat down beside him, and looked up at Veronica, he dropped his left arm out from a blanket that was covering his lap, and pet my head.

I couldn't appreciate the breakthrough in Walter's behavior for long, because something close by smelled heavenly. Before I could discover exactly where it was coming from, Walter put his scooter in reverse, and headed to his room. That's when I realized the scent was coming from the side pocket of his scooter.

I quickly followed him, my nose poking in the air, like a seal balancing a beach ball. Carla, and a few of the residents, couldn't help but stare, as we came down the hallway—curious to see what shape Walter was in, and no doubt, surprised to see me happily trotting alongside him.

When he got to his room, Walter opened the door and drove the scooter inside. I didn't wait for his permission to enter—I went where my nose led me.

Once he put a few things down on the kitchen counter, he reached into the goody bag, and revealed the source of the delicious scent—a gigantic barbeque bone. It was the kind most owners see at the pet store, and say, "Nah, that's too big."

"Here you go, boy, you earned it," he said, before handing me my reward.

I did a victory dance, prancing around the living room with my head held up, and the monster in my mouth, before taking it over to the window, where I discovered someone had placed a brand new dog bed. I plopped myself down, straddled the bone between my paws, and joyfully tore into it.

The afternoon sun was streaming down on me through the living room window, and I had something new to chew. Pure joy.

19

The good thing about being around someone who is new to dogs is that you can take advantage of them. I mean that, of course, in the best possible way. :)

Walter gave me more food over the next week—before Jane informed him that it wasn't a good idea—than I could have ever imagined.

One morning after breakfast, he called me to follow him back to his room. Once he got situated on his recliner, he opened a few peanut butter condiments he had taken from the dining room for me.

"Boy, it doesn't take much to make you happy, does it?" he said, watching me voraciously lick each one clean.

No, Walter, just something to lick, love, chase or chew,

and I'm content.

When I finished, Walter put the empty condiment containers on a small table beside him, and picked up the newspaper to work on a crossword puzzle. I retreated to my new bed by the window and watched him.

I quickly picked up that Walter had a habit of talking to himself. Either that or perhaps he felt I could bark out an answer to his puzzle.

"We're getting there," he'd say every few minutes before announcing the part of the puzzle he was working on. "California City where the Pony Express made its last ride . . . ten letters and it ends with an 'o'."

After we completed our first crossword together, this became a routine of sorts, with Walter calling me back to his room after breakfast for a visit. He would always give me a treat, or something he grabbed from the dining room, and then I'd give him moral support, while he finished his daily puzzle.

Being given lots of treats and goodies was only part of my reward for helping Walter on the night of the incident. He began taking me outside to sit on the front patio, where we watched the world go by.

SunRidge was located on the corner of a well-traveled, four-lane road, and there was plenty to see. On the corner opposite of us—on the same side of the street—there was a car wash, which included an oil change station, as well as a mini-market. Kids from nearby schools always congregated there. On the corners across the street, there were a gas station and a mini-mall.

I always loved to look out the windows whenever I visited with residents, curious to see anything that was going on, but now I was breathing the fresh air, while taking in the sights, as well as the sounds and the smells.

Walter's observations were quite different than mine.

I picked up on the sound of young kids whizzing by on their skateboards, and spotted a long, white line trailing a plane in the sky; and was fascinated by a large dancing sandwich on the street corner, promoting lunch specials.

Walter saw a changing world.

"Look at these kids today with tattoos on their necks, their backs, their calves . . . they're everywhere," he bemoaned. "In the old days, sailors, bikers, and servicemen used to have them, but one, two tops. I don't understand why these kids want to plaster their bodies with this permanent, ugly crap. Birds in a tree on your back might be hip today, but what's it going to be when you're seventy? A mistake, that's what. And it's more than just tattoos with this generation . . . you have men punching huge holes in their ears, and all kinds of other crazy piercings. Something's not right here."

Conversations with dogs are obviously one-sided, but that never stops people from talking to us, as if we could respond.

"Look at these young girls, Wrigley. What are they,

twelve, thirteen years old at the most?" he asked me, while observing a group across the street at the convenient store. "They look like they're ready to date . . . all sexed up and sophisticated like that. Jesus Christ, you have the rest of your life to be a grown-up—be a kid while you can."

Sometimes people waiting at the nearby bus stop would come over and ask Walter if it was okay to pet me. He seemed amused by all the attention a dog could get sitting next to an old man in front of an assisted living home.

One day an attractive young woman spotted me, and walked over, giddy with excitement.

"Hello, sweet thing," she said to me, kneeling down, and cupping my head with her hands. "Are you keeping your owner company?"

"He's not mine," Walter told the woman. "He's the house dog here."

She didn't acknowledge Walter, and continued to interact with me.

"You are so cute!" she told me, while I sniffed around her. "I had to leave my dog at home, when I came here to go to college. I miss him like crazy."

I kept trying to sniff at her backpack, so she took it off, and put it in front of me to explore.

"Where are you from?" Walter asked the woman.

She didn't reply. Instead she began massaging my back, while I looked up at Walter, soaking in her affection, with my tongue hanging out.

"I wish you could meet my Beagle, Sam," the young woman told me. "You guys would have so much fun together. He's with my mother, but I'm sure he's not complaining . . . she's the super-generous grandparent that spoils him rotten."

Walter tried to initiate conversation with the young woman another time, but she was too smitten with me to bother. After a few minutes the young woman walked away, but not before she gave me a big kiss on the top of my head, and thanked me for giving her a much needed dog fix.

Walter was puzzled by our exchange.

"I don't know that I've seen that before," he told Veronica, stopping at the reception area, once we came back inside.

"What did you guys see?" she asked.

"This young lady just came up and carried on an entire conversation with Wrigley, without saying a single word to me, and I'm the one who can actually talk."

Veronica did her best to help Walter understand.

"I don't know what to tell you, Walter," Veronica told him. "Maybe she thought Wrigley was a better listener than you. I'm sure she thought he was cuter."

When Walter first arrived at SunRidge, a comment like that would have gotten under his skin. But now he just chuckled and drove away.

Since returning from the hospital, there was a noticeable change in Walter. He asked for things more kindly, and said thank you when he was given something. Believe it or not, he even played Bingo one afternoon.

It was a shock to everyone, including me, when I looked up from my spot next to Tamara, where I began sitting after Marjorie left us, and watched him walk in. He didn't make a fuss about anything, and made small talk with the others in the group, who were all women that day. Unfortunately for Walter, his social skills turned out to be better than his luck, as he didn't win any of the games.

Despite his Bingo outing, Walter was still a solitary man, preferring to stay in his room and watch sports on TV. I walked into his room a few times, and he seemed happy to have my company.

It didn't take long for me to learn that baseball was Walter's favorite sport, and the Chicago Cubs was his team. If you saw him watching a game—with his baseball cap on and a scorecard in his lap—you would have thought he was a kid. He never paid much attention to me while the Cubs were playing, but one day Walter made a connection between my name and his team.

"My God, how could I not have realized this before," he said, his voice rising with excitement. "You're Wrigley, as in Wrigley Field, where the Cubs play. If a black cat walking onto the field cost them the pennant in '69, you might be my good luck dog, who finally helps them win

113

the World Series!"

Humans sure can stretch things when they want to believe something.

From then on, Walter took it upon himself to include me in the team's triumphs, and commiserate with me after their defeats. I quickly learned that with the Cubs there was a lot of commiserating.

I wish I could have shared Walter's enthusiasm for the game, but I found watching baseball—for any length of time—to be incredibly boring. It's better than golf, but not by much.

One afternoon, however, while dozing in and out of sleep during a Cubs game, I had a brainstorm that could save baseball from being so dull!

What do you think of this idea? Each team would include a mix of humans and dogs. The humans would only hit, the dogs would only field, with the exception of pitchers and catchers, who would need to be humans.

Okay, let's play ball: a human batter hits a fly ball to centerfield, and a Golden Retriever catches the ball. That's one away. The next batter hits a line drive over a German Shepherd's head, who's positioned at second base, and it bounces a few times, before being chased down by a Chocolate Lab. The runner is rounding first base, heading for a double. If the Chocolate Lab gets to second base before the human does, he or she is out. If not, the player is safe. Make sense? All you'd need to do is make the ball lighter, so it could easily be caught by a dog, and you're ready to go.

You could equip the dugouts with dog beds and chew-bones to keep the canines busy, when they're not in the field. The bullpens would be used for human pitchers to warm up, while the dogs play chase. Teams could be by dog breed or all mixed together. The possibilities are endless…

The more time I spent with Walter, the more positive effects I saw as a result of our newfound bond. He seemed calmer and less agitated when I was around. And although he probably wouldn't admit it, he enjoyed the rapport he was beginning to have with the other residents. I'm sure the incident with Corina had a lot to do with the changes, but the house dog deserves a little credit as well.

I even noticed that Walter began to imitate one of my habits. One day, while I was doing my ritual downward facing dog pose, and leaning forward to stretch out my hind legs, he said to me, "Boy, you sure must be limber with all that stretching you do."

A few days later—after I finished my stretches—I looked up and saw Walter slowly prop his leg onto the arm of his recliner, and gently lean forward.

Who said you can't teach an old man new tricks?

20

After firing Corina, Walter contemplated what to do about replacing her. He decided to take Jane's suggestion and have Sally Riggins, who worked alongside Carla during the 6:00am to 2:30pm shift, watch after him. Rudy, the private caregiver who had been working earlier in the day, changed his schedule and began helping Walter in the evenings.

Looking back on it, Sally probably would have been a better choice originally, rather than Carla. She was in her late 40's, and had the experience and resolve to handle someone with Walter's prickly personality. And Sally had another thing going for her—she was from Chicago, and grew up rooting for the Cubs.

Despite what some might have seen as a cold or tough exterior, Sally was never anything but cheerful and kind to me. She always talked about the two loves of her life—a fawn-colored pug named Winfrey, and a chocolate Lab named Duchess. I had been around Carla more than Sally, mainly because she had a close bond with Marjorie. But among the SunRidge caregivers, there wasn't a bad one in the bunch.

Even though Sally was aware of Walter's reputation for being difficult, she was brazen enough—some would say crazy enough—to broach the subject of his heavy smoking habit. The conversation came up after Walter had a coughing attack, once we returned from the front patio, where he had just finished a cigarette. It started as a couple of dry hacks back in his room, but continued until he was choking, and having a hard time catching his breath. Sally heard him from the hallway, and came quickly to give him a couple of firm pats on the back, until he was okay.

"My mother smoked up to the end of her life… literally," she told Walter, while bringing him a glass of water. "I had the unenviable task of lighting her cigarettes during her last days."

"Well, it looks like that's where I'm headed," he replied.

"You never know, you might surprise yourself, and quit," Sally responded, with an encouraging tone.

"I doubt it," Walter replied. "I've been smoking for a

117

long, long time, and people don't change. We're all hopelessly who we are… Besides, at my age it wouldn't make a damn bit of difference anyway."

"For starters, it would help your circulation," Sally offered. "And you wouldn't get out of breath so easily."

"Tell me this," Walter replied, ignoring what Sally had said. "If smoking is as bad as they say, how come I always hear about people who smoke, drink, and eat donuts every day for breakfast and live to be 100?" Before Sally could respond, Walter answered his own question. "I'll tell you why," he said, "because it's all in the genes."

"It's that, and also how you take care of yourself," Sally replied. "I'll tell you this… Doing this job, I've seen plenty of smokers who end up in real tough shape."

"Thanks for the uplifting conversation," Walter said, sarcastically. "I'm afraid we'll have to finish it some other time. My son's coming soon, and I've got a few things to do before he gets here."

Shortly after Sally left the room, Walter's son, Mark, along with his girlfriend, Michelle, visited him for the first time since the argument they had in the hallway, when Marjorie was still alive.

Mark pulled up a chair beside Walter's recliner, and the two men talked about his hospital stay, while Michelle sat on the couch reading a magazine. Seeing what Walter had been through, and that they hadn't seen one another in some time, I was surprised at how quickly the conversation

118

became tense.

In my time at SunRidge, family dynamics were the most difficult for me to comprehend. There are so many complicated emotions, and so much history involved. I've seen several family visits begin cordially, and with a word or a look, turn ugly and filled with anger. In some cases, a single argument, stemming from an old, unhealed wound can separate family members for years or forever. It's one of the sad and puzzling aspects about human relationships.

Listening to Walter and Mark, I couldn't understand all of the logistics of what was being said, but it seemed like another battle in a long war, and the issues probably weren't as big as the wall they had built between them.

Michelle did her best to act as a buffer between father and son, but she was no match for their intensity. I decided it was time for the house dog to try to diffuse the situation. I lifted my head off of my bed, and began to growl in a deep low voice. When my intended result—an end to the bickering—didn't occur, I launched into rapid bark mode.

"Damn it, shut up!" Mark yelled, glaring over at me, showing a glimpse of his father's temper.

"Look, you guys are upsetting the poor dog," Michelle said. "Try to calm down."

"Michelle, I told you, I need to discuss this with my father," Mark responded, forcefully.

The conversation between Walter and Mark quickly returned from a momentary simmer back to a boil. It was time for Plan B.

I walked over to the coffee table, grabbed a tennis ball, which Jane had given to Walter a few days earlier, and dropped it at Mark's feet. He didn't acknowledge my attempt for a game of fetch, so I nudged his hand with my snout. He finally stopped talking for a second, picked up the ball, and tossed it toward the corner of the room. After I retrieved it, Mark tossed the ball for me again, and I quickly chased it down, catching it after one bounce. Michelle cheered, and Walter commented on my impressive fielding abilities.

Shortly after our little game of fetch petered out, I went back to my bed, rolled on my back, stuck my paws in the air, and let my head dangle to the ground.

"You guys, look at Wrigley," Michelle said, laughing, before coming over to rub my belly.

"Silly dog," I heard Mark say over Michelle's shoulder.

"Looking at that," Walter chimed in. "I'd have to say dogs must not get headaches."

The conversation went on from there, heading off in a different direction.

It wouldn't surprise me, if the issues Walter and Mark had been discussing, lived to see another day—human problems are as pesky as flies on dog poop—but at least the tone was more civil when Mark and Michelle left that day.

Once they were gone, Walter became quiet and withdrawn. He sat on his recliner for a long time, staring into space, and looking sad.

I tried to cheer him up by putting my chin on the arm rest, and looking at him with a cuteness that is impossible to resist. But it was of no use, Walter was beyond reach.

He finally moved forward in his recliner, pushed off against his cane, and stood up. I followed alongside him, as he slowly made his way into the next room. He sat down on the side of the bed, put his hands on his knees, and closed his eyes. For a second, I thought he had fallen asleep. Then he reached over, opened the drawer in his nightstand, and pulled out a small photograph. I found a spot below his dresser, and sprawled out on my side.

I watched as Walter slowly rubbed his fingers across the photograph, and began talking to it. "I tried my whole life to please you, but I never could," he said, defeated. "You pushed me so hard, but when I did well at anything, there was no praise, no pride, no love. Only criticism of how I could have done better. My biggest regret in life is that I went to work for you after college. That was my chance to break away. I wanted to get a job in advertising, but you insisted that you needed me in the family scrap business. All those awful, wasted years at each other's throats. How many times I wanted to leave, and I should have, but eventually I had a wife and kids to feed, so I stayed, and I paid dearly for it."

Walter stared at the photograph for a moment, with

tears welling up in his eyes, and then began to speak again. "It would have made such a difference in my life, if you could have told me just once that I was good enough, that I made you proud. I tried my damnedest not to be like you with my sons—to catch myself when I treated them the way you treated me—but I failed."

Walter began to sob heavily, and I could feel his emotions turning to anger. He closed his hand, making a fist, and crushed the photograph.

"Why does a father denigrate and belittle his own son, his own flesh and blood?" he asked, his voice trembling. "Why? God, tell me, why?"

When I got up, and went to Walter, he was hunched over, facing the headboard with his elbow on the bed. I gently leaned against his leg to let him know I was there. He put his left hand down, and rested it on my shoulder.

After a few moments, Walter wiped his eyes with his shirt sleeve, gathered himself, and walked back into the living room. He stood by the window, looking out, lost in thought.

"I guess the pain of some things never goes away," he said, turning back toward the living room, "and all you're left with is the torture of time to think about them."

Walter walked over to his CD player, pushed the play button, and classical music filled the room. He went back to his recliner, closed his eyes and fell asleep.

21

My most exhilarating experience at SunRidge came from out of the blue. I was asleep on my bed in the front office, when I heard the sound of Walter's scooter. I opened my eyes, and saw him talking with Jane in the doorway. After they finished, Jane called me over to her. She was holding a black and red vest in her hands.

"Let's see how this thing fits, Wrigley," she said, draping the vest over my back, and connecting the clasp under my belly.

"Oh my God, that's too funny," Theresa said, looking on from her desk.

"I don't know if it's such a good idea," Jane responded, with concern.

"It'll be fine," Walter assured her. "What's the worst he can do?"

"What does his patch say?" Theresa asked Jane.

"My name is Wrigley. I lick, love, protect, and serve."

With the vest in place, I gave myself a good shake, and licked Jane's face. She clipped my leash to my collar, and handed me off to Walter.

"You ready, boy?" he asked me, wrapping the leash around his hand.

You could have harnessed wind energy from my tail swooshing back and forth. For a dog, there's nothing like the excitement of knowing you're about to go somewhere that you've never been before.

I walked beside Walter's scooter, and we exited the front entrance. The SunRidge van was parked a few feet away. Ron loaded Walter's scooter onto the lift, and Walter and I, along with several other seniors, got on board for a ride!

On either side of the center aisle, there were two seats in each row. Walter took a window seat, and I hopped up next to him. As we started to drive, I put my right paw on his lap and leaned toward him, in order to get a better whiff of the breeze that was coming through the small window above.

Staring out the window at the passing scenery, the route we were taking looked familiar. It was the same one the Petersons took to go to the dog park. But with a vest on, and a van full of seniors, I didn't think that was our destination. So, where were we going?

I was amped up with anticipation, getting more curious the further along we drove.

Finally, the van exited the freeway, made a couple of turns, pulled into a large parking lot, and came to a stop. Ron came back and moved me to an empty seat across the aisle. He tied my leash to the metal rail, and then assisted all of the seniors out of the van. When I was the only one left inside, I began to fear the group was going to leave me behind. But, seconds later, Ron got back on the van, and came to retrieve me.

We were all outside now and ready to go. That's when I looked up and saw that we were standing in front of a supermarket! Over the years, I had made many trips with my various owners to places like this, but unless it was a pet store, I always had to wait in the car. Now, for the first time, I was going inside!

The beginning of the experience turned out to be anticlimactic, as Walter shopped for toiletries and other household stuff. But after we got the boring part out of the way, we turned down an aisle, and my olfactory system went ballistic. Every nook and cranny of every shelf was stacked with food!

Although my vest made me feel like we were on a mission, and encouraged me to behave with a reasonable degree of decorum and restraint, I definitely had more spring in my step than the average service dog, who had been down these aisles before.

A lot of the products I had seen before in places I'd lived, or in commercials on TV, but it was amazing to see them all in one place. Now I know why they call these stores *super* markets!

We went up and down one aisle after another, passing meats, cheeses, cereals, and breads. Then we came to the pet section! Walter grabbed a chewbone for me and dropped it in the front basket of his scooter. I got as close as I could, gave it a good sniff, and then licked his hand in approval.

After a bit more shopping, we got to the end of an aisle where there was a woman handing out samples of beef jerky. Wait a minute—is this a dream, or did I die and go to heaven? The lady was tall with red hair. She was wearing a black apron with a name tag that read *Faye*.

"Would you like a sample?" Faye asked. "It's from naturally raised beef, right here in the valley."

She was talking to Walter, of course, but I was responding.

"It looks like your four-legged friend wants a piece," she said to Walter. "Can he?"

"I suppose it's okay," Walter replied.

Faye didn't have to bend over very far. I gladly met her reach, and inhaled the beef jerky without chewing. I immediately began to plead for another piece, looking up at Faye intently, then over at her tray of goodies, and then back at Faye again.

"I think we found our canine spokesperson," she said, laughing. "He seems to like our product."

"The only trouble is I bet he'd like your competitors' products just as much," Walter joked, before thanking Faye, and starting to drive his scooter away.

Before he could get very far, I began to whimper.

"Wrigley, none of that," he instructed me.

It's not every day a dog finds himself inside of a supermarket, standing in front of a tray of beef jerky samples. So I started whimpering again.

"Wrigley, you had a piece, now let's go," Walter told me, while tugging on my leash to move me along. I held my weight against his effort, and looked at Faye with a pout that could have melted a dictator's heart. Walter and Faye exchanged glances without saying anything to one another. I inched forward and offered Faye my paw. She leaned down, gave me a shake, and slipped me another piece of beef jerky.

Persistence is cuteness when you're a dog.

With everything on Walter's shopping list checked off, we got in one of the checkout lines. While the cashier scanned each item, the bagger, an enthusiastic boy, commented on Walter's baseball cap.

"Sir, I like your hat." the teenager told Walter. "Go Cubs!"

"That's what I say," Walter replied. "But it was a rough season."

"Well, like my Dad tells me every September, *wait until next year*."

"I hope so," Walter told the boy, as he loaded our groceries into the front basket of the scooter. "I'm afraid I don't have that many more to wait."

Back in the parking lot, Ron packed away everyone's purchases, and helped all of the seniors get situated on the van. Then we drove back to SunRidge—smelling much better than when we left.

A week later, I overheard Jane and Theresa in the office talking about our outing. It turns out that Michelle had made the vest for me, but the idea was Mark's. Seeing that I was a good thing for his father, he wanted to strengthen our bond.

Walter and Mark were no different than any hardened relationship I had seen between parents and their children at SunRidge. No matter how much hurt and anger existed between them, somewhere in their hearts there was love. Sometimes it's buried so deep they can't feel it or don't believe it, but even in their most heated arguments, I've sensed it.

22

Over the next few months, I grew closer to Walter than I, or anyone at SunRidge, ever could have imagined. Although I visited with the other residents, as I always had, Walter enjoyed, and perhaps most importantly, needed my company the most.

In some ways Walter reminded me of a shelter dog that had been mistreated, and as a result, had become mean and angry. Just like with an abused dog, I felt if I showed him love, it would eventually be reciprocated.

But love is a two-way street, and in all my visits to Walter's room, he had not crossed the threshold that closely bonds a dog with a human—I had yet to be allowed on his couch or on his bed. I realize some people aren't thrilled about having dog hair where they sit and lie, but there's a reason it's called FURniture—it was made for four-legged creatures. That's not to say that a human loves a dog any less, if they don't allow them on their couch or bed, but it's a dog's preference. It says: *what's mine is yours, and I want to be close to you.*

I tried jumping up on Walter's bed a few times, mostly when he was reading during the afternoons. He always immediately told me to get down. One time, when he was napping, I quietly hopped up and found a spot on the corner of the bed. I thought I was home free, but moments later, he opened his eyes, and I was a goner.

"Listen," he told me, after I complied with his wishes, "this is my bed . . . your bed is over there."

Any smart dog knows that the idea of a human assuming the alpha role in your relationship is wishful thinking, spread through the years by overpaid dog trainers. Human will—no matter how well motivated or coached—is simply no match for plain old dogged determination. So I knew it was just a matter of time until Walter caved in.

After the quiet approach of sneaking up on Walter's bed didn't work, I opted for jumping up in excitable bursts—when Walter wasn't on it—and then jumping off before he could say anything. An innocent, but effective human conditioning maneuver, handed down from one generation of dogs to the next.

Next, I picked a few times when I knew Walter might not respond as strongly to me breaking the rule. I would jump up, sit right next to him on the couch, and give him what I call the puppy pose—my tongue hanging halfway out, and my ears up and perky in play mode. You know the look—the one that says, *Aren't I cute? Try to resist me, I dare you.*

I dared, and incredibly, Walter still denied me. Every time.

My breakthrough finally came on a stormy afternoon when my second least favorite sound came crashing from the heavens—thunder! It doesn't terrify me like fireworks do, but it still rattles my nerves.

On that awful holiday that celebrates America's freedom, while it tortures dogs all across the country, Jane made sure to give me a pill before the festivities began, to help keep me calm. The trouble with thunder and lighting is that you can't predict when it will occur.

At the first crack of the skies, I hid beneath Walter's bed. Not being a dog person, he didn't seem to know what I was responding to.

"What's a matter, boy?" he asked, perplexed, from his bed where he was reading. "What are you doing under there?"

Moments later, another thunderous roar came, followed by a flash of light that lit up Walter's bedroom window. I retreated even further beneath the bed, and was shaking like a leaf.

Walter now seemed to sense my terror. He got up from his bed and called for me to come out from underneath it.

"Come on, Wrigley, you don't need to hide under there," he said, while I stared at his slippers. "How about I put on my shoes and we take a walk?"

If you say the word *walk* or *treat* to a dog, even if the world is coming to an end, you will get some sort of reaction.

I sheepishly poked my head out from under the bed, investigating the authenticity of his offer. Walter surprised me by getting to his knees—quickly for an old man—and clipping my collar to a leash he was holding.

Getting back up was a different story. He put one hand on the bed, and the other on the nightstand, and pushed off, but he couldn't lift himself up. He rested for a few moments, and then tried again, but his hand slipped off of the bed. After an unsuccessful third try, he grunted, and gave up.

"Old age," he sighed, staring down at me, still halfway under the bed. "The will's still there, but the body is un-willing."

Walter then collapsed himself beside me, reached over, and began scratching the side of my face. Responding to his affection, I began to shake a little less. He scooted himself closer to me, and leaned his head against mine.

"It's nothing to be scared of," he whispered in my ear.

"I promise you." He then rolled over on his side, and using his arm for a pillow, lay facing me. It was the most peaceful I had seen Walter look, since the day I walked into his room, while he was listening to music.

The room was quiet, and it seemed as if the storm had passed, until, you guessed it—the sky shook again. It scared the wits out of me, causing me to retreat and tremble again, but it gave Walter the motivation to lift himself up.

"Let's go, Wrigley," he said, on his feet and out of breath. "It's time to come out from under there."

When I didn't respond, he added an incentive.

"How about if I give you another one of those really big bones," he said in a childlike voice. "And we'll also take a ride on my scooter."

Thinking he had closed the deal, he pulled on the leash, but there was still resistance on the other end.

"I'll even let you come up on my bed, if you come out," he offered.

I can't say if this final proposition is what got me out from Walter's bed, or if I sensed that the sky had finally finished its frightening light and sound show. Either way, a promise had been made, and when Walter honored it, I gladly took advantage of it.

Looking back, if you measured Walter's decision to allow me on his furniture in smiles, it was a good one. The dog hair did bother him some, but it didn't outweigh the joy of having me closer. It also brought out a playful side in

Walter that I hadn't seen before.

One afternoon, I was fast asleep on my side of the bed, when I heard the theme to the movie *Jaws* being hummed. At first I thought I was dreaming of the countless times I had to watch that movie, when I lived with the Phelps family. But when I opened my eyes, I realized it was Walter.

He was slowly moving his cane toward me from under the covers. He would bring it close to taunt me, before retreating and making a large circle in front of me. Whenever I took his bait and tried to bite the cane, he pulled it back. This went on for a few rounds, until I caught the cane with my mouth. When I did, Walter let out a loud howl for the first time since we'd been together.

Walter was becoming more dog-like—a good thing for any human.

23

It wasn't often that the entire Peterson clan could get away from SunRidge at the same time. But on Theresa's son, Jayden's fifth birthday, they all went down to Bennett Park to celebrate for a few hours on a sunny afternoon.

I didn't know about the plan, but following Jane and Theresa around earlier in the day, I sensed something different was on the agenda. They gave me no indication, however, that I would be joining them, so I was surprised when Jane grabbed my leash and loaded me, along with a large cooler and a canvas bag, into her minivan.

Once we arrived after a short drive, I insisted, much to Jane's displeasure, on enjoying one of the best parts of any park—smelling trash cans—on our way to meet Ron,

Tamara, Theresa, her husband James, and Jayden, where they had spread out some blankets.

Jayden and I had spent some time together at SunRidge, on the occasions when his Mom would bring him to the front office for short visits. He was a cute and precocious boy with sandy blond hair and blue eyes. Like most little kids, he loved dogs.

When Jane and I went over to greet him, I licked his face and he giggled. After Jane leaned over and gave him a hug, Jayden got on his hands and knees, and pretended to be a dog. We played for a while, until the boy took off chasing a pigeon.

Looking over to the center of the park, I spotted Ron and James, fifteen yards apart, tossing a Frisbee to one another. I quickly ran over and chased the orange disc, as it soared through the air, sprinting back and forth in an invigorating game of mutt in the middle. Each time the disc landed on the ground, I snatched it up, and celebrated by running around with the Frisbee in my mouth before spitting it out, so they could toss it again.

When the game ended and the group sat down to eat, Jane put my leash back on to keep my nose from wandering where it shouldn't be. My only salvation was a stiff breeze that sent smells of turkey and chicken wafting through the air, from the sandwiches being enjoyed.

Before everyone finished eating, Jayden, who was getting restless, asked his Mom if he could take me for a walk. Theresa tied my leash around the boy's hand, and gave him a few instructions, before letting us go.

You go every which way but straight when you're walking with a small child, which suits a curious dog like me just fine. Jayden was having a good time, and I had my nose to the ground, sniffing whatever came in our path.

At one point, Jayden stopped walking and decided I could be a horse, as well as a dog. When he climbed on top of me, I hoped he wasn't going to want a ride, because I didn't think I could carry him very far. Instead, he wrapped his arms around my neck and hugged me. Kids can be so sweet.

After a few moments, Jayden got off of me, and we continued on our way. When I looked up again, we were at the foot of a hiking trail. Theresa called over to Jayden, and told him to turn around and come back. He acknowledged her with a wave before leaning down to pick up a stick. Then he drifted up the trail a few more feet, where something on the ground caught his attention. He took his stick and whacked at the object. It quickly uncoiled and began to move.

I had never seen a snake in person before, but I had seen a show about reptiles on *Animal Planet*, and knew they could be dangerous.

When Jayden lifted his arm to strike the animal again, I moved between the snake and the boy. The stick struck the snake, and it quickly lunged forward, biting me on the cheek, just below my eye. I yelped in pain and felt disorientated. Jayden started to cry, as I cowered to the ground. The group must have heard the boy, because everyone immediately rushed over to us.

"Oh my God, it's a snake!" Theresa screamed, quickly picking up Jayden, and carrying him away.

"Go get one of the blankets!" Jane yelled to Ron.

Jane knelt down beside me, and comforted me with the same soothing voice she used the first time I met her at the shelter. "Everything's going to be all right," she told me, while slowly stroking my coat.

Ron returned with a blanket, and he and James gently lifted me onto it, and carried me to the backseat of Jane's minivan. As we started to drive, I felt as if someone was filling my head with air. It was becoming harder for me to breathe.

That's the last thing I remember.

When I woke up, I felt a steel table beneath me, and saw a vet standing above me. It wasn't Dr. Sager. It was a lady with curly brown hair, and I could feel her hand on my face. Her name tag read, *Dr. Cranston*.

I didn't think Jane was in the room, but after a few seconds, I heard her talking with Dr. Cranston.

"I'm glad you brought him in immediately—dogs can die from snake bites," the doctor told her. "We've treated him with an anti-venom. He's going to be okay."

That was the good news.

"We'll need to keep him here, depending on how he does, for at least two days," she went on to inform Jane.

And, that was the bad news.

Two days in veterinary purgatory, confined to a small, cold cage—except for short walks around the parking lot —with a view of an examining table and cabinets, and kept in a room full of unhappy, sick dogs. Luckily, I was dead to the world on the first night, and didn't even know I was there.

The following day, when I was brought back into one of the examining rooms, Jane was there to greet me. Slowly making his way behind her was a surprise guest—Walter. Out of breath, he sat down on the wooden bench along the wall. After Jane got down and gently kissed my wound, Walter called me to him. I wobbled over, and stood stiffly, as he gently rubbed beneath my neck.

"A rattler got you, huh boy?" he asked me.

I looked up at him, unable to do much, but stand there with my big blubbery head.

"He looks like a cartoon character with all that swelling," he said to Jane.

"He's still cute as ever," she replied, reaching over to wipe the crust out of the corner of my eyes. "Aren't you, Wrigley?"

I didn't know how I looked, but I know how I felt: unsteady and sore.

Jane and Walter stayed for a few minutes, doting on

139

me, and talking with Dr. Cranston, until one of the vet tech's came in to take me back to my extravagant accommodations.

I felt a little better each day, and the staff told me I was healing quickly. I could feel the swelling around my wound beginning to deflate.

Two days after my accident, just like Dr. Cranston had promised, I was ready to go home. It couldn't have come a second sooner.

24

The reception I received when I came back to SunRidge almost made the awful experience of being bitten by a snake worthwhile, if that's possible. The residents and the staff were thrilled to see me, and it felt good to be missed and loved.

My swelling was almost completely gone, but I was still a little slow. Over the next couple of days, Jane and Theresa kept me in the front office to keep an eye on me, and make sure I didn't over-exert myself.

On my first afternoon back, Walter stopped by to see how I was doing.

"Wow, he sure looks better," he told the ladies, standing in the doorway. "It shouldn't be long before he's back to normal."

I got up, and walked over to say hello. He reached his arm down to pet me, and I slipped inside of his embrace.

"They took good care of him," Jane said, looking up from a stack of papers at her desk. "And I have the bill to prove it."

"With the cost of healthcare nowadays, there's two emergencies for every emergency—the incident itself and the massive bill they stick you with afterward," Walter replied.

"It's okay," Jane responded. "There's nothing I wouldn't do for this dog."

A few days later, when I was feeling better, Walter came by again—this time to fulfill the second part of the promise he made the day I hid beneath his bed in terror. I walked over to his scooter, and he patted his hand on his lap for me to step onto the platform. I hesitated at first, wondering if it was really okay for me to hop on board.

"He might need a treat, Walter," Theresa suggested.

"No, he'll come," Walter replied, confidently. "This is a promise I made to him."

"I see," Theresa responded, amused.

"Let's go, boy," Walter encouraged me again. "What are you waiting for?"

I stepped onto the scooter, fitting snuggly between Walter and the front steering column, and away we went . . . the old man and the house dog he once hated, cruising down the hallway.

Our destination was the courtyard, and once we got there, Walter unclipped my leash. I marked a few of the bushes, and then looked up to see that Walter was holding, of all things, a Chuck-It in his hands.

"Ok, you ready, Wrigley?" he asked me, slowly raising the plastic arm extension, which cradled a tennis ball above his head. "Go get it, boy!"

The ball landed a few yards away. I trotted over, picked it up, and brought it back to the side of Walter's scooter.

"Gee whiz, that hardly went anywhere," he said, dismayed with his throw. "What doesn't old age rob you of?"

Walter tossed the ball for me a couple of more times, about the same distance, and I returned each one. Frank, the SunRidge landscaper, spotted our casual game of fetch and came over. He asked Walter if he could borrow the Chuck-It, and proceeded to hurl the ball to the edge of the property. I eagerly jolted after it, quickly bringing it back for another toss. On Frank's next throw, I brought the ball back most of the way, before settling on the grass to gnaw on it.

"A dog's life…" I heard Frank say to Walter. "It sure looks good some days."

"You're not kidding," Walter agreed. "It's hard to believe he can get so much pleasure from a fuzzy green ball."

With the ball in my mouth, I rolled onto my back. After Frank walked away, Walter drove his scooter over to me, reached down with the Chuck-It, and scratched my belly. Ahhhh . . . one of my favorite things in life—having a ball in my mouth and getting my belly rubbed at the same time.

Later that night, after I left John Stokely's room, and was heading back to my bed, I was surprised to see Walter sitting alone in the dining room. He called me over, so I took the liberty of crossing the imaginary boundary line.

When I reached him, he began to slowly, repetitiously pet my head, as if he was trying to pacify a restlessness inside of himself.

"Wrigley, I dread going back to that room and trying to sleep," he finally said. "Last night was a real doozy . . . I must have counted every sheep twice, in every farm in the country."

Walter told me to stay, while he slowly got up and walked over to the counter by the kitchen. When he returned, he was holding a bowl of cereal with milk, and a handful of dry cereal, which he spilled onto the table. As he fed me one piece after another, he continued telling me his woes.

"During the daytime I'm distracted, but my troubles always find me in the quiet of the night."

Who needs rest, I thought to myself, happily crunching on another bite of cereal—eating beats sleeping anytime.

After Walter's supply of cereal ran dry, he got up to go back to his room. I followed alongside him. It was the only time I had been in his room at night, other than during the incident with Corina.

When we walked into his bedroom, I watched as he pulled two long candles from his nightstand drawer and placed them into metal holders. Then he turned off the lights, lit the candles, and got into his bed. I hopped on after him, and made myself comfortable.

"Jane caught me doing this once, and she gave me hell," he said, as he stacked a couple of pillows on his lap to bring a book closer to his face. "I told her I've been reading mysteries this way, since I was a young boy. Some habits stay with you forever."

After Walter read for a while, I rolled onto my back. It took him a couple of pages to realize I was hoping for a belly rub. But when he noticed me, he reached over, grabbed the back-scratcher beside him, and put it to good use.

25

The slower pace of living at a place like SunRidge can sometimes fool you into believing that time is barely moving, but it steadily, silently marches on.

Summer faded away after a flurry of 90 degree days in late September. Autumn came and went quickly, as it always did, with the trees putting on their annual color spectacular, and then steadily shedding their leaves. There was now a cold in the air, and a feeling that another winter was fast approaching.

I don't mind the cold weather, it invigorates the husky in me, but I don't like it when the time changes. It always signals the beginning of the end of taking longer walks after dinner with Jane or Theresa, and playing in the courtyard until dusk, chasing balls or just hanging out. Also, the end of daylight savings confuses my internal clock. The first few days after the time gets pushed back, I always stand at my food bowl wondering why I'm not being fed.

But before winter arrived, Halloween came around. The night reserved for ghosts and goblins was mostly an uneventful holiday at SunRidge. Seniors, of course, are way past the days of dressing up, and candy is off-limits for the house dog. Except for some of the staff members, who wore costumes, and a couple of decorations sprinkled around, you would think it was just an ordinary day. The nicest part about the holiday was when a group of kids from a nearby church stopped by a little while after dinner to say hello to the residents, and get some candy.

Before the Peterson's adopted me, I celebrated Halloween with several different owners, but they weren't very much fun.

When I lived with the Phelps family, the parents let me go trick or treating with the kids, and I got lots of attention and even a few dog treats along our route. However, the night turned horrible, when a group of teenagers lit off a loud firecracker a few feet away from where I was standing, and I freaked out. For the rest of the night, I kept wildly darting off with every sound I heard. Finally, the parents took me back to the house, put me in my crate, and covered it with a blanket.

During my time with Norm and Tracie—even though

they didn't have kids—they went all out in turning their place into a haunted house. The kids in the neighborhood loved it, but Norm ruined the night for me by putting a cardboard building on my back that said *Poop Factory*. Everyone thought it was funny, but I felt stupid and uncomfortable.

A few days after Halloween passed, Jane took me with her to the hardware store to get some things in preparation for winter. Definitely not as exciting as a trip to the supermarket, but I enjoyed riding the wind in the front seat of her minivan.

While Jane asked the sales clerk a few questions about patio furniture coverings, I sniffed both sides of the aisle in search of something more interesting than bland boxes. When she got what she needed, we headed with our shopping cart to the front of the store.

In the long checkout line—leading to the only available cashier—a teenage girl behind us asked Jane to hold her place. When she returned, she was holding a small bag of popcorn! To my surprise and delight, she began feeding me piece after piece, behind Jane's back.

Hearing me happily chomp away, Jane eventually turned around and told the girl, "Please, don't give him any more."

I looked up at the girl with my tail brushing the cement floor, confident a dog's desire was stronger than a stranger's request. She looked back at me with a smile, held out her open palms, and uttered the two worst words in the English language, when spoken in succession: "No more."

On our way back to SunRidge, Jane gave me a little lecture about my food intake. "You need to slow down, Mr. Chowhound," she told me, while I looked back at her with a blank stare. "Unfortunately, your stomach can't always handle everything your eyes desire. God knows the last thing we need now is another vet bill."

Jane, I thought by now you understood that food for a dog is like sex for a teenage boy—it's always on your mind.

26

Jane's timing to buy coverings for the outdoor furniture proved to be perfect, when days later winter arrived early and delivered a wallop.

When Veronica and I walked out to the courtyard the following morning, I could hardly believe my eyes. It snowed in the valley, but never very much, and it usually melted in a few hours. This was different.

The white stuff was packed high everywhere you looked. Jane's recently covered patio chairs, now blanketed in snow, looked like ghosts. The gazebo looked like a miniature winter chalet, with icicles dangling from the roof. Not long ago I was lying on my back in the green grass, bathed in sunshine—now I was standing amidst a winter wonderland.

Humans, like dogs, need unexpected surprises. They help to offset the monotony of life. I wouldn't say the residents at SunRidge responded to the huge snowstorm like a bunch of six-year-olds, staring out of steamed windows, rearing to frolic and play, but winter's first flurry was a refreshing sight.

"How beautiful," Sandi Schifman observed, looking out one of the living room windows to the courtyard. "All we need now is some Bing Crosby music."

"Isn't that something?" John Stokely asked aloud. "I haven't seen that much snow in years. So long as I don't have to drive in it, it's all right by me."

An hour or so after my breakfast, Veronica took me outside again. A few members of the staff were out there as well, clowning around and throwing snow balls at one another. Veronica tossed me a tennis ball, which sank into the snow like a buried treasure. I excitedly dug it up, and pranced around with it in my mouth, before finally letting her have it back. While I waited for her to throw the ball for me again, I spotted a snowman in the corner of the courtyard that Jamie, the kitchen manager, had just finished making. I dashed over, jumped up on my hind legs, knocked the poor guy to the ground, and snatched his long nose, which turned out to be a carrot.

Jamie took the destruction of his creation in stride, and everyone laughed, including a few of the residents, who were watching from inside.

The next day, even though the snow still covered much of the courtyard, the walkways had been cleared, and the novelty of the storm had already begun to fade. When I awoke from a nap in front of the living room fireplace, I took a loop around the building. I found Walter's door open, so I walked inside.

He looked tired, but happy to see me. I sat next to him on the couch, falling in and out of sleep, while he looked over some papers. When he finished, he got up and grabbed my leash from a hook by the door. I hopped off of the couch, and joyously danced around, until he signaled for me to get back on it, so he could more easily clip the leash to my collar.

"At the rate I'm going, Wrigley, if I leaned over to you on the ground, I'd fall over and stay there," he told me, grimacing in pain.

As we headed down the hallway, I made sure to restrain myself and stay beside Walter's new walker, which he had recently gotten to replace his cane. He stopped a couple of times to catch his breath, and sat uncomfortably on the seat of the walker. Considering it was still freezing cold outside, I was surprised when I realized we were slowly making our way toward the courtyard.

Once we got there, Walter reached into his coat pocket, and grabbed a cigarette.

"The cold air feels good," he said, breathing out a

mixture of smoke and mist. "It helps to clear my head."

Just then the door opened behind him, and I saw Sally shivering, with a look of disgust on her face.

"Walter, come back inside," she told him, adamantly. "It's not a good idea to be out there in these conditions."

"I'm fine," he responded, taking another drag from his cigarette.

"Please, finish quickly and come back inside," she urged him again, before closing the door.

"It's a devil of a habit," Walter said, staring down at his cigarette. "I've had one of these in my hands every day since I was fifteen years old, Wrigley. I hated it the first time I tried it… Those are the things in life you have to fear like hell, because once you're hooked, you're in big trouble."

I was getting restless standing there, so I started to move around. Walter had my leash tied around his hand, so I couldn't go far.

As Walter finished his cigarette, the sun broke free from behind a bank of clouds. Nearby, I heard a bird chirping, and I moved behind Walter, spotting the tiny creature, which had landed on the branch of a small bush next to the building. Walter turned to go back inside, but my leash was tangled around his walker. He tried to untangle it, but when he turned to see where the leash led, he fell over toward the bush.

At first I didn't think Walter had fallen hard, but when I

leaned over, I saw a large gash on his forehead. I took a quick sniff at the blood coming from his wound, and then backed away from him, until my leash was free from the walker.

Just as I was about to start scratching on the door for help, Sally opened it. Unlike the night of the incident with Corina, Walter had his nurse call button around his neck and had activated it after he fell.

Sally rushed to Walter's side, knelt down, and asked him a few questions before running back inside. When she returned, Jane was with her. While Sally called 911 from her cell phone, Jane tended to Walter. Seconds later, Theresa came outside, and took me back to the front office.

Once she unclipped my leash, I paced around anxiously, before following her command to lie on my bed. Shortly afterward, I looked out into the hallway and saw the paramedics hurry by, and minutes later pass by again—this time with Walter on a stretcher.

I wished I had just sat patiently by Walter's side, until he was ready to go back in, and done nothing else. But dogs get restless and curious. I didn't know if the accident was my fault or not, but I knew my role at SunRidge was to help, not hurt, and I felt bad about what had happened.

27

During my time at SunRidge, I had become used to waiting for residents to return from various medical procedures. But this was different, because I was involved with the accident that sent Walter to the hospital.

To make matters worse, early the next morning, while I was lying on my bed, I overheard Ron talking to Jane about Walter's fall.

"I don't know if it's a good idea to keep Wrigley here any longer," he told Jane, while standing beside her desk, drinking a cup of coffee.

"It wasn't anyone's fault, Ron, accidents happen."

"But Wrigley's had his fair share. Maybe he's just not a good mix any more with seniors, who are fragile and accident prone."

"Listen," Jane said, adamantly. "Do you know how much that dog means to the residents here? Look at Walter. Wrigley has performed a miracle with him."

Ron shrugged, turned away, and left the office. I never heard anything more on the subject after that.

For the rest of that day and into the next one, I kept a low profile, mostly hanging around the front office and the reception area, sleeping for long stretches, and waiting for Jane or Theresa to take me on my routine walks. I didn't visit with any of the residents, and didn't interact much with the caregivers, or any of the other employees.

You might say I was depressed. Luckily, the good thing about being a dog is that something as simple as an un-expected treat, a long walk with fresh smells, or making a new friend, can pull you out of a sour mood in a heartbeat.

That's exactly what happened the following afternoon, when a new resident named Bee Henning moved into SunRidge. I felt such an instant, strong connection to her, I thought maybe Marjorie had sent her. Happily, the feeling turned out to be mutual.

After Bee finished going over a few things with Veronica, I followed alongside, as Jane took her to her room. Sensitive to what had just happened with Walter, and perhaps recalling her recent conversation with Ron, Jane made sure it was okay for me to stick around.

"Bee, please let me know if the dog is a bother," Jane

said, before we got to Bee's door. "I can take him back to the front with me, if you'd like."

"No, actually the person who recommended SunRidge to me told me about Wrigley," Bee replied, looking over at me with a smile. "It's one of the reasons I came here."

Score one for the house dog.

I always liked to welcome new residents, whenever possible, because I knew my presence—around those who wanted it—could help ease the anxiety, ambivalence, and often times sadness, they felt when moving into an assisted living home. It was one of those hard transitions in life that a dog can help soften.

After Jane left, Bee began sorting through her belongings, trying to make sense of where things were.

"A friend's going to come later to help me with all of this," she said, looking at a tall stack of boxes, "but I might as well get busy doing something."

She opened a small box beside her, and pulled out a few things she needed. When she came across an envelope of photographs, a smile spread across her face, and her eyes lit up.

"That's Jim," she said, holding up the picture for me to see from where I was lying, a few feet away. "We met on my first day of high school . . . he was a senior. I remember my father saying I should be with someone my own age, instead of a boy who was about to graduate, and go off to college. But I knew he was the one for me. It was hard having a long distance relationship those first few years, but it was well worth it in the end . . . we had such a wonderful life together." Bee paused and silently reflected for a moment before continuing. "I can't say I thought it would end this way. With all of my ailments, we both assumed I'd be the first to go . . . but here I am. When they say love lasts forever, that means even after the person is gone. I miss him so much, Wrigley. But I know he'll be waiting for me when God decides my time here is done."

Bee slowly shuffled through the remaining photographs, stopping at a couple of them to tell me stories. Once she finished, she stared out the window, and I sensed a sadness coming over her. She called me over to her side, wrapped her arm around my shoulder, and began to cry.

"It's going to be okay," she reassured herself, after releasing me from her embrace. "You'll help me through it, right, Wrigley?" I wagged my tail, and sat down. Bee reached over to pet my head, and when she felt the moisture from her tears on my fur, she started laughing. "Look at me," she said, "we just met and I'm slobbering all over you. Isn't it supposed to be the other way around?" I lifted my paw onto the arm of her wheelchair, and she put her hand over my paw.

"Well, I guess this is home," she said, scanning the room, and allowing the reality of where she was to sink in. "I can't say I was in any great hurry to get here. I asked the driver if he didn't mind taking a detour on our way over. It turned out to be a twist on *This Is Your Life* from the back seat of a taxi. We went by my first job at the movie theatre, the ballroom where I used to dance as a young girl, then to the restaurant where Jim took me on our very first date, and finally through the neighborhood where we lived as newlyweds. None of the places look the way they used to, but I still see them as they once were. I don't know when I'll have the chance to get by them again, so I'm glad I did. Believe it or not, Wrigley, the driver didn't even charge me for the ride. What a sweet, young man."

Bee finished talking, and closed her eyes, as if she was trying to gather strength. When she opened them, she looked over at me and said, "It's been a long day, and I need to get some rest. If you're not here when I get up from my nap, we'll see each other again real soon . . . okay?"

Not long after Bee lay down, Jane came by to check on her, and found me staring out the window. She called me to come, and closed Bee's door behind us.

28

The next morning, when Jane came to work—before she put her things down—she walked over and gave me a big hug.

"My best friend's Golden Retriever, Chloe, died last night," she told me, looking upset. "I just want you to know, Wrigley, how much I love you."

She then grabbed my leash, clipped it to my collar, and told Theresa we would be gone for a while. We got into her minivan, which was idling outside the entrance, and drove until we reached her friend, Karen's house, fifteen minutes away.

After she rang the doorbell, Jane looked down with a sad expression on her face. "I hate that silence," she said to herself, "when you're expecting to hear a barking dog."

When Karen opened the door, her eyes were red, and you could feel a heavy sadness coming from her.

"I'm so sorry," Jane told her, reaching over to give her a hug.

"Thanks so much for coming over."

"I brought Wrigley with me... I thought he might help."

Karen got down on her knees, buried her head in my coat, and hugged me tight. "He looks great," she told Jane, getting back to her feet. "I haven't seen him, since he got bitten by the snake."

"Please, don't remind me—what a horrifying experience that was."

The three of us walked into the living room. Karen and Jane sat on the floor with their backs against the front of the couch, and I lay on my side close by.

"The last month was so hard for her ... I'm glad that at least she's no longer in pain," Karen told Jane, "but I miss her already."

"Of course you do, it's a huge loss," Jane responded, reaching over to take Karen's hand.

"I wish dogs could live a little longer, and humans could live a little shorter," Karen said, looking over at me.

"Are you trying to put us out of business?" Jane joked.

"No," Karen replied, smiling.

"I'd be happy if dogs lived longer," Jane responded, "but I'm not so sure I want to give up any of my years."

"I probably feel the way I do, because I don't have kids," Karen offered.

"Maybe so."

"Would you mind if we walk to the end of the street?" Karen asked, as she stood up. "I'm sorry, it's hard for me to sit still for long."

"Of course not," Jane answered. "Wrigley, do you want to go for a walk?"

I quickly got to my feet, and stood wagging my tail, while Jane put my leash back on.

"I just want to go down to the grass bluff," Karen told Jane. "It was one of Chloe's favorite spots."

We walked a short distance, and along the way passed a couple of barking dogs in their front yards. When we got to the bluff, we crossed paths with a short-haired woman, who was walking a super-spunky Chihuahua that was missing its left eye. Jane asked the dog's owner if it was okay for me to say hello.

"Definitely, this is Giuseppe," the woman said proudly.

"I've seen you guys before," Karen said to the woman, while leaning down to pet Giuseppe.

"Aren't you the one with the Golden?" the woman asked.

"Yes…" Karen managed to say before starting to cry.

"She passed away last night," Jane said, speaking for her friend.

"Oh my gosh, I'm so sorry, she was such a beautiful

162

dog," the woman responded.

"Thank you," Karen replied.

"I know how you're feeling . . . I lost my Chocolate Lab six months ago, and I'm still devastated. Every time I walk down here with Giuseppe, I think about Roscoe. We spent twelve years together. He was by my side through so much . . . divorce, two surgeries, and a career change. He's gone, but I still feel him here," the woman said, putting her hand over her heart, and getting teary-eyed.

The woman leaned over and gave Karen a hug. When they separated, she unclipped Giuseppe's leash, and the little guy and I ran around together. Small dogs sometimes irritate me because they get nervous around dogs my size, and they bark at their own shadow. But Giuseppe had the spirit of a big dog. When his owner threw him the ball, he was after it in a flash. He looked so funny with a big ball in his tiny mouth. I tried to pry it from him, but he would have none of it, easily darting away from me every time.

When Giuseppe ran off with his owner, I sniffed around for a while, leaving my mark on a few fragrant bushes before rejoining Karen and Jane, who were sitting together on a nearby wooden bench.

I found a spot on the ground in front of them, and watched as people passed us by on the walkway. Not long after, Jane told Karen she had to get back to work, and we slowly made our way down the block again.

In Karen's doorway, Jane wrapped her arms around her friend for a long embrace, and then we got into the minivan and drove off.

29

Once we returned to SunRidge, I crashed on my bed for a few hours. When I woke up, and walked out into the hallway, I came across Sally. I happily went over to her, and when she reached down to pet me, I smelled Walter's unmistakable scent of cologne mixed with cigarette smoke.

I followed Sally, as she headed toward Walter's room, hoping that he had returned during my nap, or while Jane and I were visiting Karen. Just before we got to his door, I realized that Mark and Michelle were a little ways behind us. I waited for them to reach us, and greeted each with wags and sniffs. After Sally chatted with the two of them for a minute, she headed across the hallway into Ellen Lubuck's room, while the three of us walked in and found

Walter resting on his recliner.

"Well, if it isn't the whole welcoming crew," he said, looking over at us.

"Hey, Dad, how are you feeling?" Mark asked him from across the room.

"I suppose I'm in good shape for the shape I'm in," he answered. "Damn glad to be out of that place, I'll tell you that much."

Mark and Michelle walked over to opposite sides of Walter, while I sniffed around his feet.

"I'm glad you're back," Mark told Walter, reaching out to put his hand on his father's shoulder.

"What exactly happened, Walter?" Michelle asked.

"I took Wrigley out with me to have a cigarette, and then, I don't know…"

"We'll call this episode, *Two Stooges in the Snow*," Mark joked, leaning down to give me a scruff on the head.

Walter and Michelle both laughed.

"Dad, we brought you a turkey sandwich from the deli, if you're hungry."

"Thanks, I'll have it later. I have to rid my system of that hospital food first."

"That bad, huh?" Michelle asked.

"Let's put it this way, if I were there for any length of time, I'd starve."

"I can't remember where, but recently I read that hospital food is much better than it used to be," Michelle replied.

"Well, apparently the change hasn't reached where I went . . . you know it's a bad sign when you're using a spoon for your vegetables."

"Michelle," Mark interjected, "keep in mind you're talking to a man who never had a meal he didn't complain about. If there were a dictionary for descriptive terms, under *picky eater*, you'd find a picture of my Dad talking to a waiter about something."

"That's not true," Walter responded, meekly defending himself.

I followed Mark as he took the brown sack with Walter's sandwich to the refrigerator.

"It looks like you have a friend, Dad, who's willing to help you, if you can't eat the whole thing," Mark said, noticing me trailing him.

"Oh, I bet he will," I heard Walter say behind me.

"He's such a great dog," Michelle said, greeting me with a smile and a pat on my head, when I returned to the living room.

"I can't remember, Mark, did we have a dog when you were growing up?" Walter asked.

"Yes, Dad," he answered, sounding slightly annoyed. "Remember after you left the house, I came home from school one day, and discovered Mom and her new boyfriend had given the dog away."

"What!" Michelle responded, shocked. "Why did she

167

do that?"

"She said she was having a nervous breakdown and couldn't deal with anything," Mark answered.

"Sounds like your mother," Walter responded.

"Let's talk about happier things, shall we?" Michelle suggested.

"Dad, did you hear about the trade the Cubs made?" Mark asked.

"I caught the tail end of them talking about it on ESPN in the hospital."

"I'm telling you, next season they have as good a shot, as they've had in a long time, to finally doing it."

"I'll believe it when I see it."

"I guess I can't blame you," Mark replied. "I don't think either of us ever recovered from 2004. I still can't believe they were five…five outs away from the World Series, leading three to nothing, and lost eight to three."

"Remember what I told you when you turned to me and said 'Dad, we're five outs away?'"

"Yeah… Never count outs. How can I forget?"

"An old gambler's rule. Unfortunately, it proved to be prophetic."

Somewhere during the conversation, I fell asleep. Baseball is hard enough to watch, but listening to people talk about it is beyond bearable.

I opened my eyes when Mark and Michelle were getting ready to leave. Mark walked over and wrestled me for my Kong toy before he shook his father's hand and said goodbye. Michelle gave Walter a hug, and then reached down to give me one as well.

Even though Walter didn't say anything to me about it, I could tell he was happy with Mark and Michelle's visit. It was the only one I had witnessed, where there wasn't any real friction between him and his son.

A little while after they left, Walter got up from his recliner and walked over to the refrigerator. He stared inside for a few moments, contemplating what to eat. Sensing it might be time for his turkey sandwich, I repositioned myself to the edge of the kitchen. Just then, he closed the door, and walked away empty-handed.

Why do humans do this? You have all this incredible food staring at you, and the free will to eat it, and you turn away without having anything? It's unbelievable.

Instead of eating, Walter put on some music, and went back to his recliner. I sat beside him, and he reached over to pat my head. The room was dark now, except for the last rays of daylight, which were slowly surrendering to nightfall.

"Another day…" Walter said, taking a deep sigh and looking out the window, as the sun sank behind the mountain. "I guess you have to be grateful for every one you get, when you get to where I'm at."

30

The next morning after breakfast, Walter called me back to his room to keep him company, while he worked on a crossword puzzle. Even before we got to his room—on our walk down the hallway—I sensed a restlessness in him I had never felt before.

Once he settled into his recliner, he began having a difficult time concentrating on the crossword puzzle. He kept picking it up, and putting it down, and getting up and staring out the window, and then pacing around the room. Something was obviously eating at him. I sat on my bed and watched him, wondering what it could be.

At one point, when his eyes met my gaze, he called me over to the side of his recliner. "Listen, Wrigley," he said, pausing to look out the window before continuing to speak. "I want to let you know that I'm not going to be around much longer. They ran some tests on me, when I was in the hospital, and found out that I have pancreatic cancer. I wanted to tell my son yesterday, but I just didn't have the heart to. It's not that I don't think he can face the fact that I'm going to die soon, but I hate to be more of a burden than I've already been."

Walter seemed a little less agitated after he told me the news. He picked up his pen and crossword puzzle, and looked to find where he had left off. A second later, he dropped his hands to his lap, looked over at me, and said, "I know it's strange telling a dog this kind of stuff, but I had to get it off of my chest, and if it's possible for you to understand, I wanted you to know. Also, I wanted to thank you for being my friend."

Walter then retracted the foot rest on the recliner and signaled me to come closer. Once I was directly in front of him, he leaned forward as far as he could, and wrapped his arms around me. Once he released me, Walter got up, and without the aid of his walker, slowly made his way to the kitchen. When he returned, I was sitting and waiting for the peanut butter treat he had in his hand.

Walter didn't speak about his illness to me again, but over the next week I saw him leave SunRidge often, and return with a pensive look on his face and paperwork in his hands. I assumed he was coming back from doctor appointments.

When Walter finally told his son about his condition, he did so over the phone, while I was lying beside him on the couch. The words that were coming out of his mouth— *terminal, cancer, death, hospice,* and *funeral*—normally carry with them great emotion, heaviness, and dread. But Walter delivered the news to Mark like a weatherman announcing a sunny day with a slight accumulation of clouds by nightfall. After he finished answering what sounded like a series of questions from Mark, he put down the phone. Looking exhausted, but relieved, he rested his arm on me, closed his eyes, and fell sleep.

Early the next morning, Mark and Michelle arrived at SunRidge, and before going to see Walter, they stopped by the front office. While they discussed Walter's medical situation with Jane, I aggressively worked on a new rope toy.

As you can imagine, living at a place like SunRidge, I've heard many conversations about illnesses, surgeries, and treatments. I always listen long enough to find out what's going on, but as soon as someone mentions *chances of survival,* I do my best to tune out. It's not that I don't have faith in doctors, or their ability to assess a person's medical situation correctly, it's that statistics can't measure a person's will to live, and they don't allow for the possibility of miracles—and as the house dog, I've seen my fair share of those.

Before I stopped listening to Mark and Michelle's conversation with Jane, I did find out more about Walter's medical history. The combination of Type 2 diabetes—which I knew he had from his daily insulin shots—and a lifetime of smoking, had made his circulation so poor that, according to his doctor, he risked having one or both of his legs amputated. Before coming to SunRidge, he had undergone two surgeries—the first for a Carotid artery, and then another a year later, to remove a buildup of fluid from around his heart. According to Mark, both procedures took their toll on Walter. The recovery from the last one was especially slow and hard, with the pre-surgery anesthesia taking a long time to pass out of Walter's compromised kidneys, which caused him to have hallucinations for months. Adding advanced pancreatic cancer to a man in Walter's general health created a very difficult, if not dire, scenario.

By the time Mark and Michelle left the front office, their hearts were heavy. I tried to cheer them up by playfully galloping alongside them on their way to Walter's room, but they were too deep inside of themselves to notice.

When we arrived at Walter's door it was closed, which was hardly ever the case, since the incident with Corina. Mark held Michelle's hand, turned the handle, and they went inside. When I tried to follow, Mark held up his hand to signal that I wasn't welcome.

I pried my nose in the sliver of space between the door

173

frame and the door, trying to smell what I couldn't see, and then retreated to a spot a few feet away.

In a matter of minutes, after closing my eyes, I found myself staring up a tree and barking at a large squirrel, which was on the top branch. He was nervously chirping away, looking for an escape route, but there wasn't one. At last, I had a squirrel up a tree, with no power lines, fences, rooftops, or other trees around! I was prepared to wait him out for as long as it took.

At that moment, Michelle opened the door, jarring me awake, and, unfortunately, bringing me back to reality. She motioned it was okay for me to come inside.

After I stretched, and gave myself a good shake, I followed Michelle into the bedroom, where Walter was lying awake in his bed. Mark patted the mattress for me to hop up, but I was already in mid-flight when he did so. I sniffed around a bit, and then sat beside Walter, looking over him like a doctor with a dangling tongue, instead of a stethoscope.

"Hello, Wrigley," he said, looking up at me. It was the first time I had seen him that day, and his eyes looked as though he hadn't slept much.

I leaned down and gave him a couple of quick licks on his face. He reciprocated by reaching up to scratch the side of my head.

"Walter, I've never met any of your doctors," Michelle said, looking on from a chair she had pulled up beside

Walter's nightstand. "But when it comes to bedside manner, I bet this dog is better than any of them."

"He's definitely less expensive," Mark cracked. "And he makes house calls."

Despite the lighthearted moment, the mood in the room was somber. Sensing that Walter's time was limited, the tone of Mark and Michelle's conversations with him began to change.

"Is there anything you haven't seen or done in this life, Walter?" Michelle asked, later in their visit, as casually as possible.

"Nothing I can think of," Walter answered.

"What he doesn't experience in this life," Mark interjected, "he'll get to do in the next one, when he comes back as a bird."

Walter let out a chuckle. "You still remember that, huh?"

"Yep, I even remember the spot we were at when you told me," Mark replied.

"A bird, huh, Walter," Michelle said, surprised. "What kind?"

"Oh, I don't know. A hawk or an eagle would be nice."

There was a knock on the door, and Sally poked her head inside. "I need to get in here for a minute. Do you mind?" she asked.

"No, it's fine," Michelle told her.

"I'll be quick, I just need to do one thing."

"No problem, take your time," Mark told Sally. "We're just discussing the afterlife."

"Oh boy, I better get out of here as soon as I can," Sally responded.

"If you could come back as anything, Sally, what would it be?" Mark asked her.

"I'd have to think about that one." Sally replied, "My first thought, with the day I'm having, is that one life is more than enough."

"I'm with you, Sally," Michelle replied.

Mark and Michelle stayed for a little while longer, waiting until Walter fell asleep to leave. Once he did, Mark gently lifted me off the bed, and called me to follow him and Michelle back to the front office. They chatted with Jane for a few minutes, before telling her they would return sometime in the morning.

When they arrived, I was already in Walter's room, digging into a new chewbone. Mark quickly turned on a football game and found a spot on the couch near Walter's recliner. Michelle sat on the other side of him, while she knitted a sweater for her niece. Walter hadn't said much all morning, and didn't appear to be feeling well, so I was surprised when he became animated about the game.

"Just catch the damn ball and stop with the show-boating," he barked at one of the players. "This fool's celebrating after catching a fifteen yard pass, when his team's down by two touchdowns."

"He's happy," Michelle innocently chimed in. "What's wrong with a little joy?"

"Next thing you know," Walter went on, ignoring Michelle's comment, "they'll be tweeting after they catch a pass."

"It drives me crazy." Mark said, agreeing with his father. "That, and when they stand over a guy after a tackle, taunting him."

"Well, Wrigley," Michelle responded, looking over at me, on my bed. "I guess I'll keep my mouth shut from now on."

When halftime of the game came, Mark stood up, stretched his arms above his head, and announced to the group, "It's probably a good idea for us to go now."

I perked up when I heard the G-word, getting to my feet. Mark and Michelle began moving around quickly, which gave me the feeling something out of the ordinary was happening. I stood and watched the two of them, looking for clues.

Michelle headed to the kitchen and took food from the refrigerator, and put it into a cooler, while Mark pulled a few things from Walter's hallway closet. Then, both of them helped Walter out of his recliner, and wrapped him up like a mummy in warm clothes and a blanket. When Mark walked over to pick up my water bowl, and grabbed Marjorie's box of peanut butter biscuits, I got super excited. Michelle grabbed my leash from the hook by the door, and I obediently sat, as she clipped it to my collar.

Michelle, Walter, and I waited, while Mark left and returned with a wheelchair. Once Walter got situated in it, and was ready to go, the four of us slowly made our way past the front office—where Michelle waved back at Jane and Theresa—and out the front door.

When we got to Mark's car, he and Michelle carefully eased Walter out of the wheelchair and into the passenger seat. Michelle then opened the back door, and I jumped inside.

I immediately smelled hamburger, which I took as a good sign. Cars are notoriously a great place to find fast food leftovers, chips, nuts, or cookie pieces. I put my nose down, and began searching around me.

"Go ahead, Wrigley," Michelle encouraged me, allowing me to move to the other side of her, "I don't think you'll find much."

She was right—all sniffs, no snacks.

God I hate it when people are neat freaks.

31

We drove for quite a ways before getting off the freeway and climbing a steep, winding road. As we zigzagged back and forth up the hillside, I was reminded of a similar ride I took as a puppy in the back of a truck that caused me to get sick, while we were in motion. It wasn't a pretty sight when my owners came to get me and discovered my mess.

When the car finally came to a stop, I waited while Mark and Michelle helped Walter back into his wheelchair. Michelle opened the back door, grabbed the end of my leash, and led me out.

Wherever we were, it sure smelled good. I stuck my snout in the air, and took in a few good whiffs.

Michelle wrapped my leash around her wrist a few

times, and then, alongside Mark, who pushed Walter, we made a slow procession to a lookout point. Once we got there, I curiously inched forward, and Michelle quickly pulled me back.

We were standing on a plateau between two cliffs, partially covered in snow. The canyon below was a mix of large rock formations, rugged terrain, and trees. A long ways down, I could see a body of water snaking through the canyon.

"Well, Dad," Mark said, taking in the view, "if for some reason you come back as a pitcher for the Cubs, instead of a bird, this will give you the feeling of being one."

"The Cubs can always use pitching, so that wouldn't be so bad," Walter joked. "But this is incredible."

"I love nature in the wintertime." Michelle said, squatting down, and resting her arm on Walter's wheelchair. "It's so pristine and beautiful."

"And, best of all, uncrowded," Mark added.

Off to the right in the distance, I spotted an object in the sky. Mark followed my gaze.

"You guys check that out, way over there," he said, pointing. "What an awesome spot to hang glide."

"You couldn't get me in one of those things for any amount of money in the world," Michelle responded.

"I bet if you tried it, you'd love it," Mark replied. "Remember, you promised to go ziplining with me."

"I will," Michelle answered, "as soon as I can get my

nerve up."

The conversation trailed off, and everyone gazed out at the natural surroundings. Other than an occasional gust of wind, there was no movement or sound. I turned my head from side to side, looking to spot something of interest, but when I couldn't, I decided to lie down.

Nobody said a word, until Michelle spotted a pair of hawks circling high above us. "Look!" she exclaimed, standing up to point out the birds.

"Here you go, Dad," Mark said, handing Walter a pair of binoculars, and wrapping the strap around his father's neck.

"Can you imagine being able to soar like that?" Walter asked, marveling at the birds in flight. "Listen closely and you can hear that beautiful sound of their wings gliding through the air."

"I hear it," Michelle replied.

"Oh to be a bird, flying weightless and free," Walter said, taking the binoculars away from his face, and letting them rest on his chest, "instead of an old, broken down man in a wheelchair, waiting to die."

"Speaking of birds," Michelle said, quickly pivoting away from Walter's comment about dying. "I can't believe how many geese I've been seeing on my morning jogs. I love hearing the honking sound they make when they fly through the sky . . . they sound so happy."

"Do you know why they fly in a V formation?" Walter

asked her.

"I used to know this, but I forgot."

"It forms a slipstream, so that the birds further back in the formation exert less energy when they fly."

"The only thing I remember about geese is that they mate for life," Michelle replied. "A woman doesn't forget things like that."

"I think they live for 20 to 25 years, so that's longer than most relationships," Walter said.

"Did you guys know that if one of them gets sick or shot, a pair of geese will drop out of their formation and stay with the injured bird, until it can fly again or until it dies?" Mark asked.

"I didn't know that," Walter answered.

"That's so endearing," Michelle responded. "Now I like them even more."

I hate to break up this love affair with geese, but I will anyway. I'm afraid these people are overlooking a few things. First of all, when these birds aren't flying, they're shitting all over the place. Secondly, while they're sitting around shitting, they occupy open spaces, where people and kids walk and play.

I remember a park that I used to go with Tracie, and during certain times of the year, geese took the place over. They finally had to turn it into an off-leash area for dogs, so we could get rid of them. The only redeeming qualities about these birds are that they're fun to chase, and dried goose poop can be pretty tasty.

From geese, the conversation shifted to a trip Mark and Michelle were planning on taking to see polar bears in Manitoba, Canada.

After a half hour or so of listening to everyone talk and staring out at the scenery, I was beginning to get bored. I poked my nose at Walter's arm, and he freed it to pet me from beneath the blanket that was covering him.

"Did you guys bring those treats for Wrigley?" he asked Mark and Michelle.

"No, I left them in the car, but I'll go grab them," Mark offered.

"It's all right," Michelle replied. "It's getting dark, and I'm getting cold. What do you guys say we head back?"

"Have you seen enough, Dad?" Mark asked Walter.

"Yeah, I'm ready to go." he answered.

32

After we loaded into the car, Mark turned on some music, while Michelle helped Walter adjust his headrest, and draped another blanket over him. Everyone was situated and ready for the long trek down the hill, but the humans, who are often the ones guilty of having short memories, forgot one thing—my treat!

I nosed around the canvas bag Michelle had beside her, and looked up at her, as if to say, *I think you forgot something*. She reached inside, opened the plastic bag, and handed me a peanut butter biscuit. After I finished it, I curled up and dozed off, thankfully missing the winding road the second time around.

When the car came to a stop, I opened my eyes, and

stood up. We were at the bottom of the mountain near the freeway. Mark turned to Walter and asked, "Do you have enough energy, Dad, to take a quick drive through the old neighborhood?"

"Too late," Michelle answered with a laugh, hearing the first wheezes of Walter's infamous snoring. She gently lifted his head, and put a pillow beneath it, so he wouldn't be leaning against the hard window.

"I think I'll drive there anyway and surprise him," Mark told Michelle.

Within ten minutes, we were off of the freeway, and on a boulevard lined with shops and restaurants. Michelle cracked one of the back windows, so I could get some air. I immediately picked up the scent of a dog close by, and looked around until I spotted an exuberant Lab riding the wind in the car beside us. There was a small child in the backseat, who was trying to get her dog to notice me, but the pup was too content to care.

I continued staring out the window, looking at the scenery of passing cars and people on the street, while listening to Mark and Michelle reminisce about places from their high school days that were no longer around.

When the boulevard came to an end, we made a left turn, and found ourselves alongside a large cemetery.

"That's where my Grandfather is buried," Mark said, looking over to see if Walter was still asleep.

"I didn't know that," Michelle replied. "So is my Mom's

Dad."

"After he died, my Dad visited his grave every couple of weeks, just to make sure he was still dead."

"You're kidding me. How long did he do that for?"

"I don't remember… I think it was almost a year," Mark replied, sadly.

After passing the cemetery, we transitioned onto an open two-lane road, bordered by hillside.

"If you don't mind, I'm going to drive up to my childhood house," Mark said, looking at Michelle in the rear-view mirror.

"That's fine," she replied. "Your Dad's still sound asleep."

With nothing interesting left to look at, I curled up beside Michelle, and rested my head on her lap.

"Isn't this the stretch where your brother was hit on his bike?" she asked Mark, looking out her side of the car.

Mark didn't respond.

"I'm sorry," Michelle said, leaning forward, and reaching her hand around the head rest to rub Mark's shoulder. "I know it's hard for you to talk about. It must have been devastating for your family."

"It's okay … if we're going to be together, you should know about it," Mark finally responded. "Jeff's death sent my father over the edge. He was hardened already, but this turned him to stone. The anger ate away at him for years— he just couldn't let it go. My mother tried to deal with it differently. She eventually met with the guy who hit Jeff, in hopes of finding some closure. It helped a little, but I know losing one of her sons shortened her life."

"The guy was drunk, right?" Michelle asked.

"Yeah, it happened on a Saturday night. My brother and his fiancé were training for a race they were going to ride in Paris during their honeymoon. The guy was three times over the legal limit."

"It's so sad."

"The thing that still gets me," Mark said before pausing to catch his emotions, "is that Jeff had finally found this great woman, who shared his passion for cycling … they were a week away from moving in together, and then this."

"Oh my gosh, I didn't know that," Michelle replied.

"For years I wished it had been me," Mark continued. "Jeff was my Dad's first born and his favorite. They were so similar, saw eye to eye on everything. I was the rebellious one, always at odds with him. I think my father turned his anger toward me because Jeff was gone, and I wasn't what he wanted me to be."

"I'm so sorry, honey."

Seconds later, Walter began to move in his seat. He cleared his throat, and said, "I'm sorry."

"For what?" Mark responded anxiously, looking over at him. "I didn't think you were awake."

"For being the way I was after your brother died," Walter replied.

"I appreciate that, Dad," Mark responded, "but our relationship suffered from more than just that."

"I know," Walter replied sheepishly.

"Really?" Mark said, unconvinced. "When it comes to things like this, you've always been clueless."

"We're having such a nice day," Michelle interjected, "let's try to keep it that way."

"Michelle, please … stay out of this," Mark responded, getting agitated.

"If you're going to get into it with your father, Mark, pull over right now," Michelle said adamantly. "I don't want to be in the back seat, while you're driving angry."

Mark found an open spot on the right side of the road, and pulled the car over.

The car fell silent, and the longer it stayed that way, the more uncomfortable everyone in it became. I could feel Michelle nervously shifting in her seat beside me.

Finally, Walter began to speak. "Listen, I know you aren't happy with the father I was, but unfortunately, I can't change that now. I didn't want to be like my old man, but that's who I became. I've hated myself and everyone around me for most of my life because of it."

Mark leaned back against the headrest and didn't respond.

After staring straight ahead for a few moments, Walter reached over and put his hand on Mark's wrist. "Son, I want you to know before I die that I love you," he said softly, turning toward him. "I know it's a small consolation for the father I wasn't, but it's the best I can do."

It looked as if Mark was going to say something to his father, but instead he leaned forward, put his head in his hands, and began to sob.

"I waited a long time to hear that," he said finally.

"Well, I don't have a long time left to say it, and I'm glad I finally did. I only wish I had said it sooner."

"That makes two of us."

"You could say it again if you want, Walter," Michelle suggested, trying to add a little levity to the moment.

"Okay, I'll even do one better . . . I love both of you."

"Thank you, Walter. I love you too," Michelle said.

"And," Walter added, "I think the two of you should get married."

"What?" Mark responded, stunned. "When I told you I was getting married the first time, you said—in front of my future wife—that marriage is the biggest mistake a man can make."

"Can't a dying man have a change of heart?" Walter responded.

The car was still thick with emotion, but it felt as if a long pent up damn had finally broken.

Michelle scooted up to the space between the two front seats, and put her arms around Mark and Walter, bringing them close together. When she moved away, the two men stayed connected for a long embrace.

"I love you, Dad," I heard Mark whisper.

By the time Mark and Walter separated, their eyes were filled with tears.

I had been quietly watching the monumental moment unfold. It was time for me to become part of it. I made my way behind Michelle, and squeezed between her and the passenger seat. I turned toward Walter and began licking his face.

"Wrigley!" Mark said, slapping his hands against the steering wheel. "I almost forgot you were here." I lunged across Michelle and slurped his face.

"I'm insulted, Wrigley," Michelle said to me. "Everyone gets a kiss but me?" She stuck her face out, and I licked it repeatedly. "Thank you, sweet boy," she said, smiling.

Everyone was emotionally exhausted and hungry. Michelle handed Mark and Walter protein bars before opening the cooler and setting aside a cup of yogurt for herself. Once they finished their snacks, Mark started the car and we got back on the road.

"I have an idea, Dad," Mark said, scooting me off of the center console. "Why don't we go to the batting cage for old-time's sake? You can watch your star second baseman hit a few."

"I think I can make it a little while longer," Walter replied.

"Are you sure you're up for it, Walter?" Michelle asked.

"If it's not for too long, I should be okay."

A few miles down the road, Mark spotted a sign that read *Billy's Bat-A-Way*, and pulled into the parking lot. When we got out of the car, a young boy behind a gated area in front of us, was hitting balls thrown by a machine. One pitch after another, the boy swung and smacked the balls back against a large net. It was definitely more exciting than watching baseball on TV!

"Well, let's see if I still got it," Mark said, returning from inside the building with a bat in his hands.

"How long has it been?" Walter asked him.

"I can't remember, maybe ten years or more."

When his turn came, Mark traded places with the young boy, and raised the bat off of his shoulder. The machine hurled the first pitch, and Mark swung and missed. The ball hit the net just beyond where we were standing, and it scared me to death. Michelle leaned over and massaged my head to comfort me.

"Just warming up," Mark shouted out, reassuring himself.

The machine spit out another ball, and Mark hit it on a line drive to the back of the net.

"There we go—double off the left field wall," Mark said proudly.

"Good swing, but I think that would have been foul," Walter said, taking a lighter from his sweatshirt pocket and lighting a cigarette.

"See what I grew up with, Michelle?" Mark said, quickly

looking back at us before the next pitch came. "Dad, you're crazy—that was easily fair."

Michelle leaned over to Walter and whispered, "Just let him hit, Walter."

Walter kept quiet the rest of the time, until Mark finished and walked through the gate to rejoin us.

"Any calluses?" he asked, looking at Mark's hands.

"No, I'm fine."

"You looked good in there."

"Thanks, Dad."

"For an old-timer."

Mark shook his head and grinned, and then began wheeling his father back to the car.

33

The final stages of life for a resident and his family can be like riding a roller coaster without being able to see where the tracks lead. The ups and downs, and twists and turns can be frightening and difficult to navigate. Walter's journey was no different.

He began chemotherapy for his cancer, and while the doctors were hopeful that he had the strength to withstand the treatments, it turned out that he didn't have the stamina or the will to continue.

As he told Mark and Michelle during a visit after one of his treatments, "I just don't have the energy for a fight I know I'll eventually lose. If it's my time, I'm ready to go."

For a while after his decision, Walter was able to

continue his normal routine at SunRidge with the help of the caregivers, and frequent visits from Mark and Michelle. But it soon became clear that Walter was steadily declining, and that a better option for him would be hospice care. Walter was opposed to the idea, not wanting to adjust to new people being around him. After a long conversation with Jane, Mark and Michelle decided to take him into their home, so that he could live out his final days. Once he got settled, they would hire a hospice nurse to visit every couple of days to keep Walter comfortable. Mark and Michelle asked the Petersons if I could join them until Walter passed, and they agreed.

It was strange to be away from SunRidge. Except for the night I spent at Theresa's house—after Walter was abused—it's where I had been for a long time. Luckily, dogs easily adapt to new environments, and it didn't take me long to get used to living at Mark and Michelle's suburban home.

Michelle pampered me like a new mother, keeping me busy with a steady stream of chewbones and toys, and brushed my coat regularly. Each morning she took me jogging with her, and I made friends with other dogs along our route. During the day she worked from home, which allowed her to check on Walter and me often. When Mark came home from work, he would visit with Walter, and then toss the ball to me in the backyard, or wrestle with me on the living room floor. After dinner we would all gather around Walter's bed in a room set up for him, and watch old movies and sports.

Michelle set my bed beside Walter's on a small riser, so it was easier for him to be close to me. With Walter becoming more fragile, she felt it was best for him to have a space separate from me.

There was only one part of the living arrangement that was not totally agreeable. Mark and Michelle had two cats—Midas and Moses. The first few days after I arrived, they both cautiously circled around me, like a prison guard would with an inmate. I tried to engage them a few times, but it was beyond them to interact with a lowly dog like me. They sure are arrogant critters.

As the days wore on, Walter spent more and more time sleeping, and for the most part, his waking hours were foggy and filled with pain. I did my best to comfort him, even though at times I wasn't sure he knew I was there.

In the rare moments Walter was lucid though, he would return to his old self.

One night, Mark and Michelle were gathered around Walter's bed, watching TV and waiting for the President to make his State of the Union speech. I was far more interested in something else—a large bowl of popcorn sitting on Mark's lap. When he noticed my intense gaze, he tossed a few pieces of popcorn on the ground, which I quickly scrambled for. Just as I looked back up at him for more, I heard Walter blurt out, "Why the hell do they have to do that?"

"Do what, Dad?" Mark asked him.

"Why does this idiot need to tell us what the President's going to say before he says it?" Walter asked, irritated. "Can't we wait five minutes to hear it in his speech?"

"I like it," Michelle responded, looking up from a stack of papers on her lap. "It gives me a quick gist of everything, so I don't have to watch the whole, long boring thing."

"It's a different world, Dad" Mark offered, as he got up to bring the empty popcorn bowl to the kitchen.

"Well, it may be different," Walter replied, "but it sure as hell ain't better."

In a short period of time, Walter became less and less responsive to everything around him. Physically, he was still beside me every morning when I woke, but his eyes were dim, and his spirit was gone.

I suspect Walter was at the point where he wished he were an old dog, and someone would prick him with a needle to end his pain and suffering. But human life takes its course on its own terms.

The strain of caring for Walter and watching him decline was getting to both Mark and Michelle. Many times throughout my stay, I would find them outside of Walter's room looking depleted and depressed. I comforted them like I did the residents at SunRidge, with good cheer and a coat to cry on.

On a rainy afternoon, Walter's primary physician, Dr. Felman, stopped by to see him. Although he perked up more than he had in several days, before the doctor left I overheard him tell Mark that Walter would more than likely pass away within twenty-four hours.

The following day, Mark stayed home from work, and he and Michelle held a vigil at Walter's bedside. The mood was solemn, but Mark shared old family stories that with the passage of time had become more sweet than bitter. They helped to fill the difficult passing moments, until the inevitable came.

Hearing is the last sense people lose when they're dying. Selfishly, as a dog without words, I've always wished it could be touch. If it were, Walter would have felt the warmth of me lying beside him, with my head tucked inside of his arm. And he would have felt Mark and Michelle, on opposite sides of the bed, holding each of his hands. And he would have felt the tears falling from Mark's cheeks onto his arm.

But as it was, the last thing Walter heard before he left this world was his son saying, "Dad, I love you."

Hours later, Walter's body was picked up and taken to be cremated, as he had requested. There was an empty feeling in the house with him gone. Michelle brought my bed from Walter's room into the living room, where I listened to her and Mark begin planning a small gathering to remember Walter's life.

The next morning, Michelle called Jane to tell her about Walter's passing, and to let her know she would be bringing me back to SunRidge that afternoon.

As I sat and watched Michelle gather up my things for our departure later that day, there was a part of me that wanted to stay and become the family dog I had always hoped to be. At the same time, I knew in my heart that helping the residents at SunRidge was my life's purpose. I had almost given up hope that I would ever find my place in the world, with all of the false starts I had before the Peterson's adopted me. I wanted each of them to work out, but for one reason or another they hadn't. I guess sometimes desire and destiny take different paths in life. And in my case, I'm glad they did.

When I walked through the front entrance of SunRidge, Veronica was the first person to greet me.

"Wrigley's back!" she burst out with joy before coming around the front desk, getting down on her knees, and petting and hugging me.

Hearing Veronica's excitement, Jane and Theresa came out of the front office. They hugged Mark and Michelle goodbye, and then enthusiastically welcomed me back.

When everything returned to normal, I left the reception area to go visit with the residents. Just as when I had returned from my snake bite, the old saying—absence makes the heart grow fonder—proved true. I relished all of their attention, and returned the favor with wags and sniffs and licks.

Bee was the happiest to see me. Her room was all set up now, and it included a dog bed, and a clear plastic jar filled with treats on the kitchen counter. Once I got comfortable beside her, she slowly stroked my coat, while I sniffed at the book she was reading. "You'd like this one Wrigley, it's narrated by a dog," she said. "I'm just about finished.

After taking a sip of water, Bee read the last part of the book aloud. It went like this…Being old isn't easy. But at the end of our journey there is still laughter, kindness, forgiveness, friendship, love, and if you're lucky, a dog to help with all that ails you.

Afterward

Three months after Walter died, as I was coming back from Bee's room to the front office, I saw Mark and Michelle standing in the reception area. They were both formally dressed. Mark was wearing a black tuxedo, and Michelle had on a long white gown with flowers in her hair.

When they spotted me coming their way, Mark patted his hand against his thigh for me to come quicker. In a flash, I was at their feet.

"Hey, boy! How's the best dog I know doing?" Mark asked, trying to pet me without getting slobber or hair on himself.

"We missed you, Wrigley," Michelle said with a big smile.

I wagged and wiggled and looked up at them with affection.

"Guess what, Wrigley?" Mark asked me, with excitement in his voice. "We're getting married today, and you're coming with us!"

"You wanna go?" Michelle asked me.

Where? When? Now?

"You can be our mutt of honor," Mark said, laughing.

The two of them went into the front office, and chatted with Jane and Theresa for a few minutes before clipping Walter's leash to my collar, and leading me out to their car.

With Mark in the driver's seat and Michelle in the passenger seat, I moved up from the back seat, and put my front paws on the center console between them.

"Honey, is that okay?" Mark asked Michelle. "Is he going to get hair all over your gown?"

"Don't worry, I'll have my Mom clean it once we get there."

"I love that you're so easy going," Mark replied, taking her hand. "It's one of a thousand reasons why I knew I had to marry you."

"You'll have to share the other nine hundred and ninety-nine with me on our honeymoon," Michelle said.

"I will," Mark replied. "And don't worry, I won't make you give me a single reason why you're crazy enough to marry a guy like me from a family like mine."

"I can name three right now," Michelle quickly responded. "You make me laugh, you make me think, and you make me feel."

Mark leaned over and gave Michelle a kiss. She smiled and glowed.

Before long we pulled up to a beautiful, old stone building. There was a crowd of people milling around outside. Mark and Michelle got out of the car, greeted a few friends, and then Mark handed my leash off to a young boy named Scott.

"Let's go, buddy," Scott said to me, as I stood intently watching Mark and Michelle walk away. "We're going to take a nice long walk, and then we'll meet up with them after they get married."

He led me to a nearby trail, which we hiked up, traversing a twisting path, until we reached the top. He sat down on a wooden bench, and I hopped up to join him.

"Not a bad way to kill some time," he said, scanning the view. "It sure is quiet up here."

I looked around, and took a few whiffs of the air. When I turned back to Scott, his eyes were closed, and he was breathing in and out slowly. I jumped off the bench, and found a spot on the ground to stretch out. I rested until Scott opened his eyes again, stared at his watch, and told me it was time to go.

We took a less windy route back down the hill, which brought us to the bottom quickly. When the trail ended, I looked up and saw people talking and laughing, as they poured out of the building. Once we got closer, Mark spotted us, and came our way.

"We did it, Wrigley!" he said, beaming with joy and leaning down to scruff my head. "Michelle and I are married!"

When Mark turned away to accept congratulations from a group of people, Scott and I walked around. He bumped into somebody he recognized and made small talk, while I fixated on the women and men wearing black bowties, who were walking around with trays of food.

After the crowd had socialized for a while, Mark stood beside Michelle, and tapped a spoon against a glass to get everyone's attention.

Scott grabbed an empty chair on the lawn, and I lay down in front of him.

Mark started his speech by thanking everyone for sharing the special day with him and Michelle, and then told sweet and funny stories about the long journey the two of them had taken to become husband and wife.

While he continued to talk, my eyes were getting tired. Just as I was about to drift off, I heard my name and perked up.

"Wrigley . . . I can't forget to mention Wrigley. He's the dog here some of you might have noticed. For those of you who don't already know the story, this dog saved my father's life and befriended him at SunRidge, where my Dad spent the last part of his life. If you get a chance, go by and give Wrigley a pet or two. He'll love you back ten-fold. Also, I want everyone to know that I found out on Monday that a portion of my Dad's money, which was defrauded in a Ponzi scheme, has been recovered. Michelle and I will be making a large donation to the shelter Wrigley came from in Walter's memory."

ACKNOWLEDGMENTS

Very special thanks to: Miki Smirl, Gayle Chin, Jennifer and Melody Ingram, Jesse Hanwit, Tamara Fielding, the kind folks at Candlewood, and last but not least, my dog, Payton, who sat a few feet away while I wrote this book, waiting patiently for break time. Thank you for being my dog—I couldn't have adopted a better one.

54344099R00128

Made in the USA
Middletown, DE
03 December 2017